"Now," Shane said, "I shall kiss you."

His words quickly brought Clair's protest. "No. You will do no such thing—"

But he did, and with force. She tried to escape his demanding mouth but it was futile. She succumbed, responding to his passionate kisses, desiring only that this moment would go on.

"So," Shane released her at last. "You do find me attractive, Clair. It's just that you won't admit it. There remains only one question. Will you marry me?"

She gasped. Never had she expected this. "I've vowed never to fall in love again—" she said firmly.

"You are in love, idiot!" he said harshly. "And by God, you'll marry me if I have to drag you to the altar!"

South of the Moon

by

ANNE HAMPSON

Harlequin Books

TORONTO · LONDON · NEW YORK · AMSTERDAM
SYDNEY · HAMBURG · PARIS

Original hardcover edition published in 1976
by Mills & Boon Limited

ISBN 0-373-02266-2

Harlequin edition published June 1979

CHAPTER ONE

Dawn hung in the African sky, mysterious as the land itself as its luminescence spread over the lonely bushveld, changing its neutral colours to gold and yellow, with occasional flashes of rusty red or streaks of fiery bronze.

Clair's pensive gaze was fixed, one half of her mind desiring nothing more than to appreciate the miracle of nature as the flaring golden sphere rose majestically above the horizon, but the other half of her mind was occupied by those momentous events which had led to her coming here, to this part of the Transvaal, with her cousin Sharon, and her friend from schooldays, Jean Baker.

Jilted at the altar. . . .

With a shuddering sigh Clair turned, left the stoep, and went back to her tiny bedroom where, unable to remain still, she paced about in a small circle, feeling like a caged lion.

If only she could forget! If by some miracle there was a magic potion she could take! But no. The whole scene kept on returning, over and over again, torturing her, bringing hot tears to her eyes and a terrible ache to her throat.

The dress, billowing out like a fairy gown; the head-dress, the orange blossom—

"No! I must stop this thinking, this continual dwelling on that terrible experience!"

But of course she could not put it from her, just as if it were nothing of any great importance.

Her parents had expended all their savings on the wedding – declaring that Clair was worth everything they could give her. And so the reception had been booked at none other than the Castle Hotel, and over a hundred guests had been invited.

Keith had never once been late for an appointment and so it naturally came as a shock to Clair when, entering the church on her father's arm, she had realized that her bridegroom was not there.

The minutes dragged by and in Clair's heart was a terrible fear. Keith had had an accident on his way to church. Such things had happened before . . . and it had happened again. Keith was on his way to hospital. . . .

"Father," she had whispered eventually, "something very serious has happened."

"Nonsense, darling. Traffic jams, I'll wager. You know what this darned town's like on a Saturday morning."

Yes, yes, it must be a traffic jam.

It was not a traffic jam. Jeremy, the best man, appeared at last, his presence increasing the uneasy stir which was already potently manifest in the church. The note was handed to Clair's father; she recalled her almost uncontrollable desire to snatch it from his hands. She recalled his face turning ashen, remembered Jeremy's husky voice saying,

"I've done all I can, Mr Duncan – but he's adamant. I'm so very sorry."

The hours and days that followed, with Clair in a state of collapse and her mother little better. Her father, trying to be brave, must surely have been crying inside. His task it was to pack all the wedding presents and return them; his task it was to go to the little semi-detached house which the couple had obtained, and take from it all that belonged to his daughter – her clothes, her books, and all those little treasured possessions that had scarcely any monetary value but in sentimental value were priceless.

No word from Keith for over two weeks. Both he and his parents were away from home, Mr Duncan had been told by a neighbour when he went to visit the house of his daughter's fiancé. A fortnight later there did arrive a letter, saying that Keith had gone to stay for a while with his aunt and uncle in Lincolnshire.

He had been visiting them rather frequently during the past three months, and Clair was naturally a trifle unhappy at the idea of his leaving her. He was helping his uncle to build an annexe to his house, and so Clair resigned herself to being on her own at the week-ends. After all, she told herself logically, as Keith was in the building trade it was the natural thing for him to offer to help his uncle.

What Clair was not to know was that Keith had met another girl down there, and that for several weeks before the date fixed for the wedding, his mind had been confused, while he tried to decide whether it was Clair he loved, or this other girl.

"If only he had mentioned it to me," cried Clair in anguish, "we could have discussed it. But to wait until the last moment before making up his mind! To leave me there, at the church, causing me such deep humiliation – oh, I would never have believed he could be so cruel!" She had been talking to Jeremy, who had called to bring back some records she had lent him. He was tensed, uncomfortable in the extreme. Keith had been his friend for years but, he told Clair, this was the end. He would never speak to him again as long as he lived.

"If only we could get our daughter away somewhere," Mrs Duncan was saying a few days later, tears rolling down her cheeks. "A complete change of scenery, the doctor prescribes. But with spending all our money on the wedding—" She broke off, wishing she had not reminded her husband of the terrible loss they had suffered. For the proprietors of the hotel had been forced to make the full charge for the wedding breakfast. Had they been notified even one day sooner, they could have made some reduction, but as things were, the food was wasted and therefore they would have to insist on payment in full.

"We might be able to take her away for a week," said Clair's father, but it was Clair herself who put this aside at the very outset.

"You're not paying out any more money for me," she told him determinedly, and she added, "One day I shall pay you back."

"We don't want money, Clair darling," said her

mother. "We want only your happiness."

Happiness. . . . Peace of mind she might one day attain — when this searing pain in her heart was healed, but happiness was not for her. Clair vowed never again to put herself in a position where she could be left, heartbroken and humiliated, at the altar. And if she was never in that position then it was logical to own that she never again intended to fall in love.

Clair's bridesmaids came to see her regularly, as did one or two other friends. But for the most part people felt too embarrassed by the whole business, and in consequence they kept away.

"It mightn't be quite so bad if you hadn't given up your job," Jean said one evening when she and Clair were together in the sitting-room. "Could you get it back, do you think?"

"I wouldn't go back to the same office and have everyone looking pityingly at me." Clair gave a shudder at the picture. True, it would pass eventually, but as she was feeling at present she knew she was quite unable to face any further humiliation.

"Your mum says the doctor's advice is a complete change?"

"He thinks you can just go abroad at will." It was Clair's father who spoke, having entered the room carrying a tray on which were two cups of coffee and some dainty sandwiches. "Doctors don't always understand that their advice can't possibly be carried out."

"He wants Clair to go abroad?"

Mr Duncan nodded his head.

"And she'd go if we could possibly afford it," he declared emphatically. "However, we can't, so we've to keep Clair here."

Clair looked up into his troubled face. He seemed to have aged ten years or more, she thought.

"I'll get over it, Father," she assured him – yet in her heart she wondered just how long it would take her to get over it.

The trouble was that she still loved Keith, and the idea of his preferring another girl was like a sword turning in Clair's heart every time she thought about it.

It was less than twenty-four hours later that Jean, having arrived almost at the same time as Sharon, came out with the news that she had been made a gift of a small farm in South Africa.

"Now I ask you," she said, spreading her hands, "what would I do with a farm in South Africa?"

Mr Duncan said,

"I take it that it's the little place your great-uncle's been working for the past thirty years or so?"

"That's right. From what we've gathered he's never made anything of it – not profitwise, that is. He's eked out a meagre living and been satisfied with that, being a bachelor, then at last he decided to sell it and come to England to retire—"

"Sell it?" broke in Sharon, looking puzzled. "You've just said he's given it to you."

"It was his original intention to sell it – so he says

in his letter which I received this morning. But no one was interested except his neighbour, who sounds a rather arrogant, pompous kind of person who's wanted Uncle's little plot of land for some time. I do remember that Uncle once wrote to us saying this neighbour had called him a cantankerous old man who ought to have been a female, so obstinate and meddlesome was he, *and* without either sense or wit."

"That's nice!" inserted Sharon, her grey eyes glinting angrily.

"So Uncle decided to be obstinate and refuse to sell out to this man – Shane Neville's his name – but instead to come to England and advertise the farm as a gift to any young person who would like to accept a challenge. He admits he didn't think I'd want it, but once he saw me he thought I could be the sort of girl who might just possess a spirit of adventure."

"And don't you possess a spirit of adventure?" queried Sharon, a curious inflection suddenly entering her voice.

"You've known me long enough to be able to answer that yourself. Yes, of course I have a spirit of adventure, but I've also got a modicum of sense – in spite of being a female," she added with a grimace. "And I'm darned sure I couldn't manage a farm by myself – especially as I'd be unable to enlist the help of my neighbour should anything go wrong. You see," she added, "the farms are very scattered, and Uncle had no other neighbour anywhere near to him."

"Ngumi Farm, I believe you said it was called?"

Mr Duncan looked at Jean, his brow creased in a frown of concentration. "That is the name?"

"Yes, that's right."

"Sounds intriguing, a name like that." Sharon's eyes were strangely fixed upon Clair's bent head. Clair was looking down at her hands, clasped loosely on her knee. It was plain to her cousin that her entire mind was elsewhere – on that cad who had let her down. "You've had some experience of farming," she added, transferring her attention to Jean.

"I was brought up on Grandfather's farm, as you know, but I've been on my own now for over three years – ever since he died and Uncle Steve and his wife took over. We didn't get on— Well, it wasn't quite that," she amended. "They naturally wanted the place to themselves, and in any case, I was ready to find my own feet, and I must own that the chance of independence was more than a little attractive."

"You've done well," from Mr Duncan. "Your little flat's a gem, and you've an excellent job as chauffeuse to old Mr Jenison—"

"No more. I'm out of work – or soon will be."

"Out of work?"

"He's decided to enter Normandy House."

"The home for the aged?" Mr Duncan looked surprised by this news. "Is there any special reason?"

Jean nodded her head.

"He's had several 'do's' as he calls them, so he's decided he mustn't live alone any longer. Normandy House offers every comfort plus the constant care of nurses and other staff. He's wise, I think," ended Jean, but there was a slight sigh accompanying her words.

"So you'll be looking for another job?"

"I've another two weeks with him, that's all."

"To get back to this farm—" Sharon spoke at last, the same odd inflection edging her voice. "Have you definitely thrown away the idea of having a go at working it?"

Jean stared at her.

"Are you crazy?" she ejaculated.

A strange, profound silence followed before Sharon said, her eyes flicking towards her cousin,

"I too have a spirit of adventure. I also like a challenge."

Mr Duncan gave a start; Clair raised her head, her interest caught at last, although not to any great extent.

"Are you suggesting you and Jean go to South Africa, Sharon?"

"I've been bored with my office job for ages. The routine sometimes drives me to distraction."

"Your parents?" began Clair. "They wouldn't want you to go to a place like that, surely?"

"Why not?" Sharon spread her hands expressively. "Look at us! My brother hitch-hiking round the world; one of my sisters on what she calls a working holiday in New Zealand, and my other sister running a boutique in Spain."

"You're roamers, that's for sure," agreed Mr Duncan.

Jean said at last,

"I'm beginning to see what you're about, Sharon."

"I guess that three enthusiastic young ladies could work that farm," she said. And she added with a grimace, "It would be quite entertaining to aggravate our dour and woman-hating neighbour."

Clair was looking at her cousin.

"*Three* young ladies?" she said, Sharon's words having penetrated sufficiently for her to have grasped their meaning. "I'm not going to Africa, so you can count me out."

"The doctor did order a complete change. ..." Mr Duncan appeared to be talking to himself, and in fact his next words were not audible at all. Clair repeated her assertion that she was not going to Africa, but she could see by their expressions that Sharon and Jean were very much taken with the idea.

How she had come to be persuaded Clair would never really know. Looking back afterwards she reached the conclusion that, being in a state of total uninterest in her future, she had found it simpler to let herself be led both by her parents and by her friends – her very dear and loyal friends, Sharon and Jean. Clair's mother had been troubled at first, but her husband soon convinced her of the advisability of Clair's seizing this chance of getting away from the pitying stares, the awkward little sentences people still devised to express their condolences, the church, the Castle Hotel and, far more important, the possibility of meeting Keith – who might just be accompanied by his new girl-friend, for Mr Duncan had been told that she was now a regular visitor to Keith's home.

Still pacing about on her bedroom floor, Clair found her reflections moving a little farther back, to the time when she met Keith. Love had stirred within her very quickly – at the second or third meeting, she believed. Before she knew it she was wildly entangled in an emotion that carried her to the very heights of happiness, for Keith had reciprocated at once, telling her that she was the one and only girl for him.

"You're so lovely, Clair," he would say, gently touching one clear soft cheek, or staring with a sort of fascination into her beautiful violet eyes, eyes that could be delightfully shaded when, embarrassed by his praise, she would lower her long silken lashes, hiding her confusion. He would kiss her then, taking delight in the way her full, rosy lips would quiver in a little tremulous action when he drew his mouth from hers. "You make me want to kiss you over and over again, just to see your lips tremble when I've finished."

She would laugh, a silvery tinkling laugh, and her eyes would reflect her laughter, and her happiness. Keith used to take a handful of her shining, russet-brown hair in his fingers and bring it to his face, revelling in its softness, and in the hint of a perfume that sent his pulses racing – at least, he always maintained that the perfume she used sent his pulses racing.

A deep sigh escaped her now as she recalled those thrilling times, and it seemed, somehow, that the final scene was but a dream, and that she must awake to find herself coming from the church on her husband's arm . . .

Clair's musing were brought to an end by sounds coming from the room next to hers. Sharon was up, splashing water over her face from the large flower-decorated bowl which stood on the small table under the window.

Clair came from her room, welcoming the chance to get away from her own thoughts. There was work to be done – unpacking and then the getting down to arranging the house to suit their own tastes.

"Gosh!" exclaimed Sharon as she came from her room, her chubby face shining from the soap and water just used upon it. "I feel as if I really belong here already! How many hours is it since we arrived?"

"About twelve."

"Is that all?" Sharon preceded her cousin to the living-room, then turned as Clair entered. "We've so much to do here, love, that there'll be no time to think."

Clair managed a faint smile. This was going to be a strain, she knew, simply because she could not go about with a long face, making things uncomfortable for her friends.

"You're right, Sharon, there'll be no time to think."

Sharon looked critically at her.

"You've been thinking already, my girl!" she declared.

"A little," admitted Clair. "It's early days yet, remember."

"He isn't worth one second's worry!"

"Perhaps one day I shall agree with you about that."

"When you meet someone else—"

"There'll never be another time, Sharon. I'm finished with men for ever!"

"I'll make a cup of tea," offered Sharon practically, changing the subject and moving away towards the little place at the end of the house that served as a kitchen. "Jean's sleeping well. Must be the lovely fresh air of the bushveld!"

"What do you mean, sleeping?" came the indignant question as Jean appeared in the open doorway. "Girls, I'll have you know that I've been abroad since sunrise! And I've observed our neighbour!"

"You have?" from Sharon with interest. "And did he observe you?"

"No; he was in a field some distance from the roadway where I was standing. He appeared to be directing some of his farm hands who were working in the middle of the field."

"What's he like?"

"Devastating!"

Sharon's eyes opened very wide.

"In what way, might I ask?" she queried drily.

"In every conceivable way," was Jean's swift response. "Like a film-star – one of those tough, outdoor types. Handsome and strong and all sinewy and lithe. Bronzed skin – which is only to be expected, of course, living as he does in this climate – and lean, clear-cut features; dark brown hair which seems inclined to wave a bit at the front. That's about all I could see from where I was."

"You certainly saw enough," commented Sharon, still in the same dry tone of voice. "It would appear that the only thing you missed was the colour of his eyes!"

Jean grinned and said she felt sure his eyes were steely grey.

"The kind that either look through you with arrogant indifference, or strip you."

"Strip?"

"I have a feeling that when eventually we meet one another he'll be able to see every angular and bony bit of my unlovely female form." Jean and Sharon laughed and Clair found it impossible not to join in their laughter.

"You've made a pretty thorough assessment," she remarked presently. "He sounds just as objectionable as I imagined him to be."

Jean nodded her head.

"He's the sort of man whose face would crack if he laughed. Perhaps he could manage a smile on some rare occasion," she added musingly, "but I rather think his smiles would be more like sneers than anything else. I'll bet you all I've got – which isn't much, I know," Jean added with a grimace, "that he'll be forever criticising everything we do on our land."

"Let him!" flashed Clair, and both girls looked at her, surprised at her interest being so deeply aroused. She had been totally lethargic all the way from England, and last evening she had gone to bed just as soon as they had decided which room each was to occupy. "Why should we care for his opinion of our farming? He isn't a god!"

"Hear, hear!"

"In any case, we'll show him we're just as competent as he is!"

"Lacking in know-how as we are," supplemented Sharon with a light laugh. "The cheek of him, saying women are meddlesome and obstinate!" She paused a moment. "Let's live up to his opinion of us—" She glanced from one to the other. "Agreed?"

"I agree," answered Clair instantly.

"And so do I," from Jean with a mischievous grin. "If we're to have the name then by all means let's enjoy the game!"

"I'm dying to meet him," said Sharon. "You were certainly impressed by his appearance."

"Impossible not to be. Superlatively good-looking men are few and far between, you must admit. Shane Neville's the kind of man you'd instantly pick out in a crowd."

"I imagine so." Sharon paused a moment. "I was about to make a cup of tea. Come into this – er – little hole here and tell me some more about this

19

superb example of masculine perfection."

With her usual grin Jean followed Sharon into the tiny, tin-roofed apartment where stood a stove of sorts, rusty and appearing to have given up the ghost long ago, since it was partly sunk into the dirt floor. A butane stove stood precariously on a rickety table whose top, made of plywood, was so uneven as to be useless as a place on which to put cups and saucers.

It was this stove which Sharon used to boil the kettle.

"You haven't said what his house is like," said Sharon when the kettle was filled and standing on the lighted stove.

"It's completely screened from the road by trees and shrubs, so I didn't even get a glimpse of it. However, I did see the name, carved rather splendidly on an ornamental board which was fastened to a tree at the end of the long drive. Watsonia Lodge, it's called."

"Sounds most impressive! I'll bet it's a veritable palace in comparison to Ngumi Farm!"

"It wouldn't have to be much at all to be a palace in comparison to this place," laughed Jean, at which Sharon instantly declared,

"I adore our little hovel!"

"Funny thing, so do I."

"It's going to be so easy to effect improvements."

"You can say that again!"

"I'm itching to get at it."

"I suppose the outside should come first. We've to

grow almost all our own food."

"I grew some lettuces once, in our back garden," mused Sharon nostalgically. "Mum declared they were the best she'd ever tasted."

Jean laughed.

"Is that tea ready yet? I'm dying for a drink. I guess I've walked at least three miles this morning. Gee, but the sunrise was marvellous! I'm going to thank you, Sharon, for your suggestion that we come here and take up residence at Ngumi Farm."

Clair, hearing this, wondered if ever she herself would thank Sharon for her suggestion. If the memory of that terrible experience faded, then yes, she would thank her cousin – but as Clair felt at present she could not see the memory fading for some considerable time to come.

"The tea!" Sharon came in with the tray, followed by Jean. "Let us sit down over a cuppa and debate on our plans of action." She glanced up at the calico-covered ceiling and pulled a face. "I suggest we get the inside reasonably comfortable before we begin to put all our energies into the outside?" She looked inquiringly at Jean. "I know you've said we must concentrate on the growing of our own food, but I don't think a week or so can make all that difference."

"Clair," said Jean, "what do you think?"

"I think we ought to make ourselves comfortable, Jean. We'll feel more settled if the place is clean and neat." She lifted a hand. "Just look at all those cobwebs."

Jean nodded thoughtfully.

"Very well. Carried unanimously. And now – what about some form of transport? Uncle says it's seven miles to Montville, which is the nearest town, so obviously we've to buy ourselves one of those station-wagon things we saw as we came along yesterday in the hired car. Uncle was so delighted at the idea of my accepting this challenge that he gave me a sum of money – I mentioned this to you both some time back, if you remember?"

Sharon grinned.

"You said you refused it at first, but the old man lost his temper, so you decided it was best to accept."

"Indeed yes! He went off into a frenzy, almost. I have a strong suspicion that he could be quite a handful if you got his back up properly." Jean was laughing as she watched Sharon pouring the tea. "Maybe our neighbour was right when he called him cantankerous."

"It was his reference to women that riled me." Sharon handed Clair her tea. "Disparaging remarks like that prove he's not at all a nice sort of person."

"It's a pity he's like that," said Jean, stroking her chin thoughtfully. "We might need his help one of these days."

"I shouldn't think we'd get it." Clair helped herself to sugar and stirred her tea. "Far better not to ask than to be refused."

The others nodded in agreement and the subject reverted to that of the house, and the renovations necessary to provide the three girls with the minimum of comfort. They decided to go into Montville and buy cleaning materials, paint and brushes, and some material for curtains and covers.

"The furniture's not too bad at all," Jean had previously observed. "All it needs is a jolly good clean with soap and water and then the application of some furniture polish."

Arriving in town some two hours later, having walked there, they went first to the café and ordered a large pot of tea.

"We'll get a taxi back," declared Sharon firmly. "I'll bet I've lost a couple of pounds in weight with all that walking! And the heat! I'm cooked to a frazzle!"

Even Clair laughed at this, and a glance was exchanged between the other two girls.

"I suggest we separate," Clair said as they drank their tea, "and each go to a different shop."

"Good idea," agreed Sharon. "Here's the list. Let's make three columns of the items."

A quarter of an hour later Clair was on her own, in the general store which, rather to her surprise, seemed to be able to supply all she wanted in the way of polishes, soaps and disinfectants.

Several people came in, and everyone stared at her, obviously wondering who she was. At last one elderly woman spoke to her, blandly asking if she was staying with relatives or friends at one of the farms.

"No," answered Clair, civilly enough, but determined to be non-committal for all that. "I'm living at Ngumi Farm."

The woman's eyes widened.

"You are? But Mr Lumley's left." A question in her tone; Clair looked into her face and decided she could like the woman.

"My two friends and I have taken the farm over. We intend to make a prosperous concern of it."

The woman's pale grey eyes flickered with amusement.

"You're all youngsters, I expect? You must be, for otherwise you'd not be so optimistic about Ngumi Farm. Tell me, dear, about the three of you. The other two are men, of course." This was a statement and Clair had to smile. But she was also reluctant to enter into details about her friends and herself; in her opinion their private business was their own. What she did not know at this early stage was that South Africans were invariably curious about any newcomers to the area. So far-flung were the farms and holdings that a little gossip now and then was diverting, providing entertainment as it passed from one neighbour to another, perhaps taking a week or more in the process, as apart from meeting accidentally when in town, the people seldom came into contact with each other. They threw barn parties on occasions, or had a film show. They met at the Club, and Clair was later to learn that there was a polo team to which their neighbour, Shane Neville, belonged.

"My friends are females." Clair turned her attention to a stiff handbrush the assistant was

24

now holding out to her, having been searching under the counter for it.

"Females!" exclaimed the woman, in so clear a voice that several people who were looking at books at the far end of the shop turned, their attention well and truly caught. "Three females trying to run Ngumi Farm! Well, that's the best I've heard in years!"

Colouring, Clair spoke to the shop assistant, saying the brush would do very well.

"I also want furniture polish and dusters, please."

"Of course." The assistant smiled, glancing at the woman at Clair's elbow. "I'll just fetch them."

"Ah, Mr Neville. Your new neighbour – or one of them." These words penetrated above the chatter of several customers – and Clair felt her nerves tingle. Shane Neville. . . . She turned, as if forced to do so, fully aware that the woman had pointed a finger while uttering the words,

"Your new neighbour – or one of them."

Clair's eyes met his. She saw that Jean's guess had been a correct one. Shane Neville's eyes were steely grey. They looked unsmilingly into hers, and there was a strange silence as a long, all-examining moment passed.

The man nodded at length, then introduced himself. Clair returned the civility, but her voice was cold; she had no time for men in general – and certainly no time for this one. He turned presently to the counter, then to the end of the store where he picked up a book. Clair found herself unable to draw her eyes away from his figure. He moved with the springing step and easy action of an athlete, his broad shoulders and narrow thighs combining to enhance the overall effect of elastic strength that seemed to emanate from him. He turned, to bring the book to the counter assistant, and Clair, impressed by his vitality and magnetism, found herself under a strange compulsion to examine his face again, noting the keen dark eyes, the angular, aquiline features, the unblemished skin, deeply bronzed by the African sun. His hair, crisp and waving and faintly sprinkled with grey at the temples, had a well-kept, newly-washed look, but it also bore evidence of being recently teased by the breeze.

Attractive. . . . Undoubtedly a man of superlative good looks and physique . . . but a hard man, since his mouth was firm, his jaw taut. His eyes too had an implacable quality – cold as steel.

His book paid for, he again nodded to Clair, bade the woman beside her a brusque "Good morning," and strode majestically from the store.

CHAPTER TWO

THE three girls met again an hour later, each loaded with parcels.

"We've found a man willing to take us home," Jean told Clair with a satisfied smile. "He's also willing to help us buy a vehicle." She went on to explain who the man was. She and Sharon had met and spoken to him in one of the shops; he farmed Tofala Ridge six miles from Ngumi. He was young and good-looking and had a twin brother who was also his partner. "His name's Bob and he's offered us all the help we might require."

"Wasn't it lucky that we should meet someone like that right at the start?" Sharon also wore a satisfied smile. Then she added, this time with a grimace, "Was he surprised at the idea of three girls tackling Ngumi Farm! He seemed dubious as to our chances of success but offered his help for all that." She looked at Clair. "I expect you, too, have had curious glances cast at you from various people?"

Clair nodded her head, told them about the woman in the store, then added,

"Shane Neville was there. He introduced himself and that was all – except for a supercilious look," she added indifferently.

Jean looked curiously at her.

"You say he was in the same shop as this woman

who asked you all the questions?"

"Yes, he was – standing right behind us."

"So he heard you telling her that three females were farming Ngumi?"

"He must have heard."

Jean and Sharon laughed.

"Well, that'll give him something to think about!" said Jean. "Bob was telling us that there isn't much in the way of entertainment here, so our appearance will provide a talking point when the farmers and others meet at the Club— It's called the Tamarisk Club, by the way."

"Will you join it?" Clair's question included them both.

"I think we all ought to join – if they'll have us, that is. It'll be nice to attend a dance now and then."

Clair said nothing; she had no desire to join the Club, but on the other hand, she was well aware that her friends believed it would do her good to join and, in consequence, she thought she might decide to do as they wished.

A week later the vehicle arrived, driven up to the front door by Bob.

"Not too handsome an object," he grinned, "but she'll do all you want of her. She was cheap, and there's a six-month guarantee with her."

He took Jean on to the road and she drove it back. Then Clair was shown the controls. Sharon, having passed her driving test only a month previously, decided not to drive it at present.

"I'll get down to it later," she said. "Bob, are you staying to lunch?"

"Sorry, but I must get back. We've a lot to do on the farm, and one of our two men is off ill."

He looked around the living-room, commenting on the improvements they had made.

"It's not as we want it, of course," Sharon told him, "but it's far more comfortable than when we first stepped into it."

He grinned. Clair, examining his features in a cursory manner, decided that the clear blue eyes spelled honesty, the full mouth compassion, the clear-cut lines of his face integrity. She felt that even if she were a man-hater, she could not have disliked Bob. He was of the harmless type, could never do to a girl what Keith had done to her. He smiled and she managed to respond.

"Which one of you is driving me home?" he asked, and it was decided that Jean should do so.

"Thank you very much for your help," smiled Sharon.

"It'll certainly make things easier for us," said Clair.

"I hope so. And if there's anything else you want, then don't hesitate to come over to Tofala Ridge. We're busy, but not too busy if you girls should need help."

"Well," said Sharon when the station wagon had disappeared into the road, "he soon got moving! I hadn't expected him to find us anything as quickly as this."

She and Clair returned to the chore of scrubbing the several pieces of brass they had found in a shed outside, and then attempting to put a polish on them.

The two candlesticks were eventually placed on the windowsill, while the coiled snake and the bell were given a home on the sideboard.

"It's beginning to look quite cosy," commented Sharon in a satisfied voice. "I'm so glad we came." She was now looking at her cousin; Clair smiled faintly and said,

"Thank you, Sharon. I might seem miles away at times, or not interested in what we're doing, but deep down inside I never lose sight of what you and Jean are trying to do for me. It still hurts abominably, but perhaps all this – the new environment and the adventure – will ultimately make me forget."

"I believe it will, Clair," returned Sharon gently. "It was a dreadful shock and naturally it will take some time to get over it. But, love, others have managed to get over such things, so I know you will too."

Clair nodded her head.

"I'm very lucky to have you and Jean, and to be here, away from it all."

"Indeed yes. To have stayed at home would never have done at all." She paused a moment. "Don't go on being grateful and all that nonsense, Clair," she said after a while. "Both Jean and I were ready for a change; this came just at the right time for all three of us."

The sound of the station wagon took their eyes to the window; Jean brought the vehicle right up to the stoep and jumped out, her fair hair flying in the wind.

"It's great!" she exclaimed as she walked into the house. "A bit shaky and she emits an odd groan now and then, but she's in fair health for all that!" She glanced around. "The brasses look nice. I never thought you'd get them up so well."

"The next thing is the floor," decided Clair. "I think we ought to paint it and then buy some coconut matting and other rugs."

"Good idea. What colour should we paint it?"

"Brown," suggested Sharon, and this was agreed upon.

"We'll go into town tomorrow," stated Jean eagerly. "There are so many things we need now we've had time to look around properly. We could do with more kitchen utensils for one thing."

"I suggest we have just one more week on the inside, then concentrate on the farm itself." Clair was at the kitchen door, having decided to make a pot of tea. "Will Bob tell us what to do with the land?"

"He promised he would," from Jean. "I myself would like to concentrate on livestock, because I've had experience of dairy farming, as you know. And I think we ought to concentrate on producing a good supply of eggs. Bob assures me that we will be able to sell those."

"There are two sheds which look fairly good to

me," said Sharon. "We could keep a few dozen hens in those."

"You know," said Jean a short while later as she took the cup of tea handed to her by Clair, "I wouldn't have missed this for anything!"

Two more weeks passed. The house was comfortable and clean and for the past week the girls had been concentrating on the outside. Sharon and Clair had surprised themselves by their apt use of hammer and nails. After a considerable amount of noise which seemed to echo for miles across the veld, the two sheds were ready for the occupation of the hens which Bob had agreed to sell to the girls. They would require to buy some more, he had said, but for the time being these would be a start.

"They're all young pullets on the point of lay," he assured them. "Another couple of weeks and you'll be cooking your own egg custards and omelettes, you'll see!"

It was soon after his visit that Clair – who had been outside when he had first arrived – began to wonder what was wrong with her friends. They had become strangely quiet, and once or twice she noticed surreptitious glances being exchanged between them. It was almost as if there were a conspiracy afoot. However, things returned to normal, and remained so for a couple of days.

And then, right out of the blue, Sharon entered Clair's bedroom one evening and said,

"Both I and Jean have an apology to make to you,

Clair—" From behind her back she produced a letter. "This is yours. Bob brought it, having collect-it – and another one addressed to Jean – from the post office. In the first instance I opened it by mistake – having the same surname as you." Sharon paused a moment, and it was clear that she was having the greatest difficulty in continuing. But at last she did manage to do so. "I'd begun to read it before I realized it was yours and not mine. Here it is, Clair, and I hope you'll forgive both Jean and me for our original decision to keep it from you."

Clair stared at the envelope being held out to her. But she made no move to take it.

"I don't understand? You and Jean decided to keep it from me? But it's only from my parents—"

"It isn't from your parents, Clair," broke in her cousin quietly. "It's from Keith—"

"Keith!" Clair's face lost much of its colour. "But—"

"That's why we decided to hold it back. We discussed the matter, decided it was in your interests to burn the thing. But then we had another discussion. What we *think* is the right thing to do is not what we *know* is the right thing to do. We know we ought to give it to you – and here it is." With that Sharon moved forward and placed the letter on the table beside Clair's bed. "You'll do what you think is best, Clair dear, but please think very carefully before you make your decision."

For a long moment after the door had closed behind Sharon Clair could only stand, frozen to the spot, and gaze with a fixed and glassy stare at the envelope lying there, on the table where her cousin had put it.

At last she picked it up, as if it were hot. Slowly she withdrew the letter, saw that it was a lengthy one, filling both sides of a long sheet of paper. She swallowed hard, aware of a choking sensation in her throat. Keith wanted her back; she knew this even before she read one word, knew it because of what Sharon had just said.

"I can't read it here. . . ." She could not have said why, but the room became a prison from which she had to escape. Crossing to the door, she flung it wide, then went out into the clear air of the garden, turning her head to see if either of the others was watching from a window. There was no sign of them and she wandered on, and on, the letter in her hand. At last she was in the road, walking in the sandy ruts, at the sides of which grew peppers and blue-gums and a few semi-nude fir trees which seemed to be holding on to life only by the greatest effort, for the ground beneath them was cracked and parched. At length, with the healthy green lands of Shane Neville's farm stretching away on either side of the road, lands watered well by the irrigation channels running through the fields, Clair sat down by a gate and, lifting the letter, she began to read.

Yes, he wanted her back. He had made a terrible and tragic mistake, for it was Clair he loved. It always would be Clair, and if she could not find it in her heart to forgive him and to begin again, then he would remain a bachelor for the rest of his life.

"I'd heard you'd gone abroad," he continued, on the second side of the paper, "and I went to your mother to get your address. Your father said he'd kick me off the premises if I didn't move quick, and so in despair I left the house where I had spent so many happy hours, respected by all who lived there. However, fate decreed that I was to have your address, for I met Suzy Fletcher and, taking pity on me, she said she would help me to get in touch with you. So she went to your parents' house and, pretending that she would like to correspond with you, she was given your address. Why, my darling, did you go so far away from me? Oh, I can understand your feelings, dear, being left at the altar like that. Indeed, I shudder now to think that I could hurt you so, you whom I love so dearly. Clair, my dearest, please write to me saying you're coming home. We'll be married within three days of your arriving back in this country, I promise. You can't run away like this, Clair, for running away never did any good at all. So, my darling, come back — soon. All my love to you, Keith."

Four kisses ended the letter. Clair put it down on a small boulder beside her, on top of the envelope which she had already placed there.

What should she do? She recalled vividly her cousin's advice that she should think carefully before making her decision.

Did she still love Keith? Yes, there was no question of this. Her love could not die so easily, for she had loved with all her heart. Her life was planned. A couple of years alone with her husband, then a family, and the thrill and pleasure of bringing up that family. There would have been no excitement to speak of, for Keith was not over-emotional; rather was he a practical kind of man, intent on improving the business and making it the most important in the area.

"What must I do?" Her voice trembled; her lips quivered piteously. So easy it would be to write back and say she was ready to forgive and forget. So blissful to be in his arms again, his lips on hers. But what of that terrible moment when she had learned that she was left, cruelly hurt and humiliated? Forget? It was not possible – no, it never would be possible. "I can't think rationally," she decided. She would not do anything for at least a week. Yes, that would be wise, for an impulsive decision would be both foolish and impracticable – and it might be one she would regret for the rest of her life.

Although her nerves were anything but calm, Clair did feel better than when she had left the homestead. Picking up the envelope from the boulder, she moved on, her mind naturally absorbed by the contents of the letter. And so it wasn't until she was almost at home that, absently fingering the envelope, she realized with a little shock that it was empty. She had not put the letter in it; she remembered this now, recalling that she had put the letter aside – on top of the envelope. Where, then, was the letter? The wind must have caught the flimsy airmail paper and carried it away! As the idea of anyone reading it filled her with shame and humiliation, she speedily retraced her steps.

But when she reached the place where she had been sitting she found no trace of her letter. Wildly she ran around, searching the little tufts of dry grass fringing the road; then she looked towards the hedge, at the other side of which several of Shane Neville's African men were working in a field of lucerne, removing weeds which had sprung up after the violent thunderstorms which had occurred a few days previously. As she watched, Shane himself appeared, clad in tight-fitting trews and a checked shirt, the sleeves rolled up beyond his elbows. Even from this far distance Clair was aware of his vitality and magnetism; he was a man outstanding, a man of arresting physique and appearance generally.

He was waving a hand, directing one or two of the men, his eyes never coming Clair's way. She continued to look around, squirming inside at the possibility of this man's finding and reading her letter. And yet she could not call out to him and ask if it were anywhere about. She could not have explained why she was so loath to attract his attention to herself. She disliked him, it was true, and she had felt awkward when in his presence for that short while when they had met in the store. But all this did not provide any logical reason why she should not call out to him now, and ask if he would have his men search around for her letter. She had a vague idea that, subconsciously, she believed he would snub her, or treat her with the contempt which he obviously felt for her sex in general.

"In any case," she murmured as she continued to gaze across into the field, "it probably isn't there at all. It would have had to be lifted quite high to be taken over this hedge." She herself was on tip-toe, but she was looking through the top branches rather than over them as they were thinner and more straggly than those lower down, and therefore it was possible to see through them. This, she surmised, was why she was not attracting Shane Neville's attention – or that of any of the men either.

After another search along the roadside and a long look at the field on the other side of the road, Clair reluctantly turned towards the homestead. The letter was gone; it could have been lifted several times by now and be a quarter of a mile away, or even more than that. It was probably in some tree, or perhaps caught in one of the thorny bushes that fringed the dry river bed. Come the rain it would be reduced to pulp, she told herself, determined not to worry about it any more. There was a hundred to one chance of anyone finding it. If they did it would be one of the men, and he, seeing nothing important in a piece of paper, would screw it up and toss it away.

Jean and Sharon were on the stoep when she arrived back at the farm, and because of the anxiety in their eyes she forced herself to smile. And she managed to inject a light note into her voice as she said,

"I've taken your advice, Sharon, and decided to think carefully before making a decision."

Relief looked from her eyes as Sharon nodded her head.

"You're very wise, love. Come and sit down; we've just had a cup of tea and some toast. Will you have some?"

"I'd love some, thank you, Sharon. But I'll get it—"

"No, I will." Sharon rose before Clair could get past her to go to the kitchen. "You've forgiven us?" she asked, anxiety returning momentarily to her eyes. Clair said at once,

"Of course, Sharon. Think no more about it." She looked at her seriously. "I'm fully aware that, from the beginning, both you and Jean have acted entirely in my interest. It was for me primarily that you came here— No, don't interrupt and say again that it was for adventure. Partly it was, but in the main you were both thinking of me. You must have had a long discussion, and decided that a move like this was going to provide what I needed in order to get over my hurt. Well, I'll tell you both here and now," she added truthfully, "that the hurt's a little less already. I've so many things to think about that I can't possibly dwell for long hours on what's happened."

She spread her hands in an all-embracing gesture, and the two girls looked out over the undulating veld and the rich vegetation that spread out to the line of flat-topped kopjes serrating the skyline. Trees and bushes rose above the grasses, one particular variety, the kameelboom, being very graceful, its branches flat and spreading like those of a cedar. The umbrella tree also grew in fair numbers, while beneath the trees flourished the gavé bush with its grey velvet leaves, the ganna bush and the hakie. Away on Shane Neville's lush green lands miles of silver grass glistened under the bright African sun, while on some of the land belonging to Ngumi Farm the vegetation was less profitable but just as picturesque – the yellow opeslag, the sama melons, the vlei grass. All contributed to the scene of park-like beauty; all shimmered and gleamed in the fierce light from above. This was the bushveld, rising and dipping and rolling away towards the distant, mysterious horizon.

"How could anyone be unaffected by such a breathtaking scene as this?" Clair smiled again, lifting her eyes to those of Sharon as she took possession of the spare chair. "Already I should miss it if I left, and that's one reason why I'm not making a hasty decision." The other reason she did not mention, that of her own emotional instability at this time. The letter had at first seemed heaven-sent, and her heart had given a little leap. But within seconds she was facing reality, facing the fact that although she still cared for Keith, she would not easily be able to forget the hurt he had inflicted upon her.

July had merged into August; the South African

winter was coming to an end, and with it the dry season. There had been a couple of heavy rainfalls since the girls had arrived, and this had helped enormously, but in any case there were a few irrigation channels on the Ngumi lands. These had been blocked with dead vegetation and other debris, but the girls had soon cleared them and, on Bob's instructions and advice, they had now begun to widen them.

They had decided on maize as their main crop, but for the present they were concentrating on growing their own vegetables and on producing dairy products for home consumption. With the help of Bob they had learned what was the most profitable way to go about this. They had their hens, and a couple of goats to produce milk. Bob had said they must have a few cows, but Jean had allowed this suggestion to pass, for the simple reason that they had no money to buy cattle.

"We're not living too badly," said Clair one day when she came up to the house with a basket of eggs in one hand and a large canvas bag full of vegetables in the other. "Today we shall be having roast chicken, peas and beans, and chipped potatoes. Then baked egg custard, with cheese and biscuits and coffee to finish off with." Her face was bronzed, her hair at the front and temples bleached a little, adding to its attraction. Her eyes were bright, her cheeks flushed with health. To her own astonishment she was learning to live again, to see the light ahead. She knew it was this country that had inspired her, that had shown her there were many things in life worth living for, and working for. She had two true friends here with her. They got along in perfect harmony, with never a sharp word or glance to mar the relationship existing among them.

Clair knew that Jean and Sharon were awaiting her decision, a decision she had kept on putting off, but she meant to face up to it quite soon. She would not commit herself just yet, though, because she had to admit that there were moments still when the picture of life with Keith was so attractive that she could almost have written back saying she would return to England as soon as it was possible for her to do so. But these moments were rare – and with the passing of each day they became rarer still. She felt almost certain that she would choose to remain here, with her friends, at Ngumi Farm.

"We're not living too badly, you say!" Jean lifted an eyebrow expressively. "We're living like lords! And all from our own efforts. I must say, though, that the climate of this sub-tropical corner of the Transvaal is super for growing things. You remember those tomatoes I threw out a few weeks ago?"

"Those that had gone soft?"

"The very ones! Well, just you go along there and take a look now. Tomato plants as big and as healthy as you like!"

Clair's eyes opened wide.

"Really?"

"You mean," said Sharon, automatically taking the basket of eggs from her cousin and placing it on the table by the kitchen window, "that the seeds dried out and then took root?"

"Germinated as easily as that."

"So we shall have tomatoes growing on our compost heap?" Clair's eyes were gleaming with a sort of amused satisfaction. "How very convenient for us!"

"That's what I mean about this place. At home you'd have to pamper the things in a greenhouse. I know, because we used to grow them for sale when I was on the farm."

Clair was unpacking her bag of vegetables; she began to prepare them, for the evening meal, while both Jean and Sharon went outside to clean out the sheds in which the hens roosted at night. Bob arrived while they were away and as he was in a hurry there was no time for Clair to go out to fetch them.

"I just thought I'd call in passing, to give you these tickets for a dance at the Club on Saturday night. I and my brother will see you there."

"Thanks a lot, Bob." Clair looked down at the top ticket, saw the price, and reluctantly murmured something about not being sure they could go.

"You see, we're rather busy—"

"Complimentaries," interrupted Bob with swift perception. "Newcomers always get them."

"They do?"

"I'm not being charitable," he said seriously. "Yes, Clair, they're free, with the compliments of the Club President."

He went off, roaring away in a cloud of dust as his

station wagon rattled over the ruts in the drive. Clair had mixed feelings about the dance. She was not at all sure she wanted to attend a function which must inevitably remind her of Keith – for he and she had thoroughly enjoyed dancing.

However, it was to transpire that she was destined to attend, as Jean twisted her wrist when removing some heavy rocks from a piece of land which the girls had decided to use as a flower-bed. And as Sharon was still not too confident about her driving, it was left to Clair to take charge of their vehicle, which Jean had christened Sally-Ann, for no reason in particular.

In long evening dresses, the three girls piled into the station wagon and drove the four miles into Montville, then through to the far end of the town where, in a grove of cypress and palm trees, the long low building of the clubhouse nestled, its lighted windows sending forth a welcoming glow on to the car-park and the attractive gardens in front of it.

Bob and his brother, Sandy, were waiting on the steps, and before very long the girls were being introduced to the President and his wife, James and Elsie Fowler who, after chatting for a while – and tactfully avoiding any comments about females tackling Ngumi Farm – they took the girls over to a small knot of people standing at the bar and Jean and Sharon found themselves being introduced to Shane Neville who, the President said, had just returned to his home after having paid a visit to some relatives in Durban.

The President and his wife then moved away and the girls were left alone with their neighbour. He spoke to them with cool civility, and all the while his eyes were on Clair who, noticing his swift glance when her name, Clair, was mentioned, was at a loss as to why his attention should now be only with her, and not the others. She recalled that when she introduced herself on meeting him in the store, she had given only her surname, Miss Duncan. He now knew she was Clair Duncan.

"How are things progressing at Ngumi?" he inquired unexpectedly. "You've all realized by now that you've taken on a lot of hard work, I expect?" Was there a hint of sardonic humour in the rich, deeply-modulated tone of his voice? It would seem that Sharon thought so too because of the swift glance she directed in her cousin's direction.

"We're not afraid of hard work, Mr Neville," Clair heard herself retort in tones as impersonal as his own.

"The farm belongs to Miss Baker, I believe?"

"That's right." Jean shrugged self-deprecatingly. "Not a prepossessing place by any means, but as a free gift it wasn't bad at all."

Shane Neville's attention was transferred to her. He seemed to be assessing her physical strength, she afterwards maintained, much to the amusement of her two partners.

"A very odd character, old Mr Lumley," he remarked with a hint of humour. "Not cut out to be a farmer, I'm afraid."

Remembering the disparaging remarks he had made about the old man, Clair found herself stung to saying,

"From what Jean has told us he was doing it for a long enough time, Mr Neville." She glanced at Jean, aware that she might perhaps have preferred to make a retort of her own. But she was looking up into the handsome face . . . a most odd expression on her own. Clair stared, unable to believe that there was actually a look of admiration in her friend's eyes. "I should have thought there was very little he didn't know about farming," added Clair, feeling she must break the strange, unfathomable silence which seemed to be caused by Jean's prolonged and concentrated stare.

Shane Neville answered coolly,

"I'm afraid the proof of his experience and efficiency lies in the results he achieved, Miss Duncan. Without wishing to hurt Miss Baker's feelings I'm bound to say he neither knew about farming nor wanted to accept advice from those who did know."

"Perhaps," said Clair after a pause, "he took advice as interference?"

"I know he could be a little trying," put in Jean, with what seemed to Clair to be a far too ready acceptance of Shane's criticism of her great-uncle. "He has a temper, that's for sure."

"What are you intending to do with the land?" asked Shane, obviously deciding it was time to change the subject.

"We thought of having maize as the main crop,"

smiled Jean, again looking up into his handsome face. "And some cotton, just as an experiment." Even as she spoke Shane was shaking his head.

"Mixed farming is what you should concentrate on. Have any of you had any experience on the land?"

"I was brought up on a farm," replied Jean, "so I do know quite a lot about the business."

"This farm was in England?"

She nodded her head.

"It was a mixed farm, I must admit." Jean paused a moment. "You advise us to concentrate on that particular type of farming, then?"

"That's what I said. You want some livestock. You've some good grazing land there – if you set about putting a little heart into it," he added, just as if he had to, thought Clair, looking disdainfully at him. Immaculate and arresting he might be, in his white dinner jacket, but the arrogance of his mouth and eyes most certainly marred his attractions, she thought.

Aware of her critical eyes upon him, he looked at her, his eyebrows lifting a fraction in a gesture of haughty enquiry. Blushing in spite of herself, Clair glanced away, anger welling up within her. What a pompous creature he was! No wonder old Mr Lumley failed to get on with him.

"We haven't any money for cattle," Jean was saying regretfully. "Otherwise we'd most eagerly accept your advice, Mr Neville, and consider mixed farming in preference to anything else."

He frowned in thought and Clair gained the impression that he was actually endeavouring to find some way in which he could assist them. It seemed that Jean was more than willing to follow his advice, a circumstance which was more than a little puzzling, since it was Jean who initially disliked the man.

He was looking away over Clair's head and she turned. More people were arriving; they came straight to where Shane was standing with the three girls. Introductions were made and Clair found herself chatting to the husband of the woman she had met in the store. Their names were Marie and Richard Kellar; they were South Africans who had originally farmed in the Karroo, keeping sheep on their thousand-acre holding. Proud of their Voortrekker stock, they were, like Shane, conscious of their status. Although friendly towards the girls, they appeared to be a trifle patronising – more owing to the girls' optimism in coming to Ngumi than with the intention of being superior. Mr Kellar was soon offering advice, was quite openly saying all the things Shane had said about old Mr Lumley – and more.

But at least he was not supercilious about women, thought Clair, recalling Shane's assertion that females had neither sense nor wit.

The dance band was playing and couples began drifting away through the high arched opening separating the ballroom from the lounge-bar. To Clair's utter amazement Shane looked down into her face, and said,

"Might I have the pleasure, Miss Duncan?" and

although she opened her mouth with the intention of voicing a polite but firm refusal, she had no time to do so as, taking her by the arm, he propelled her in the direction from which the music came.

CHAPTER THREE

His dancing was superb; Clair found herself enjoying the interlude in spite of her determination not to do so. Memory flooded in, and she was confronted with pictures of numerous happy times she had spent with Keith. They would always dance, he had stated firmly. Whether or not they had a family, they must keep up this one pleasure which they both shared. And now she was in another man's arms . . . actually enjoying the experience of matching her steps to his.

He was so tall above her, his body so lithe and light despite its obvious hidden strength. She saw glances directed at them from people sitting out, at the small candlelit tables in the alcoves running along both sides of the ballroom, and at each side of the dais on which the musicians played.

The music stopped at last and Shane led her to a vacant table; she glanced around, saw that Jean and Sharon were with Bob and Sandy, so she had no alternative than to accept the chair which her partner was holding out for her.

"I enjoyed that," he said, lifting a hand to bring the waiter to him. "You dance exceedingly well, Miss Duncan."

The praise left her cold, but she found it impossible just to sit there, her silence implying total indifference.

"Thank you, Mr Neville." And then she added, the words forced out against reluctance, "I enjoyed the dance too."

Shane's dark eyes flickered as they met hers. They moved to settle on her mouth, a soft mouth, and full, a mouth which at this moment was quivering slightly, since she was thinking of Keith, and the many times he and she had sat like this, after a dance, waiting for the drinks to arrive.

"You danced a great deal at home?" The waiter arrived as Shane was speaking and he asked Clair what she would like to drink. She told him and the waiter moved away.

"Yes," she answered then, "I did dance fairly often at home." A catch in her voice and a shadow crossing her eyes. Shane's own eyes narrowed and his mouth pursed. "We belonged to a club," she added, speaking her thoughts aloud and not realizing she had spoken until the words were out. Shane would now ask if she had had a boy-friend, she felt sure, since this was the obvious follow-on to what she had just said. But to her surprise he changed the subject almost abruptly, beginning to talk about the farm and the struggles they were facing. He was interested, a circumstance which naturally surprised her, seeing that he had such a poor opinion of women.

"Undoubtedly something can be made of Ngumi," he added, surprising her even more, because she would have expected him to have little or no confidence in the three girls' capabilities. "The land's good basically, as I've already told you. In fact, I myself would have bought the farm, had Mr Lumley agreed to sell it to me."

Clair said, hoping she sounded casual,

"You and he didn't get along, from what I've gathered?"

An expression of grim amusement settled on his bronzed face.

"Quite right, Miss Duncan, we didn't get along." Shane looked up as the waiter appeared. The drinks were placed on the table, paid for, and then once again Clair and Shane were alone. She stole a glance towards the corner table at which Jean and Sharon were seated, with the two brothers. Sharon caught Clair's glance and gave a slight grimace, as if sending out a telepathic message of sympathy to her cousin. Unfortunately this gesture was noticed by Shane and he instantly stiffened, obviously having read its meaning.

"Mr Lumley was the most obstinate man I've ever known," he added, and somehow, Clair was convinced that this was not at all what he had originally intended saying to her. In fact, she had the very strong impression that he had been more than a little concerned about her and her partners . . . or was it sympathy she had sensed in his manner? – sympathy towards herself? A strange idea indeed, she thought, as there was no reason at all why he should feel sympathetic towards her. Besides, he was not the man to be associated with that kind of emotion; on the contrary, he was cold and impersonal, concerned mainly with his estate and the efficient running of it.

"I expect Mr Lumley wanted nothing more than to be left alone." Clair spoke mechanically, aware that her companion expected a response to his comment. "Some people are like that."

Shane's grey eyes sought hers, a brittle quality in their depths.

"If that were the case, then he had his wish," he said curtly.

"You decided not to have anything at all to do with him?"

"Yes, Miss Duncan, I decided not to bother with the man at all." His steely grey eyes looked directly into hers. "Perhaps you, too, would prefer to be left alone?"

"We would like to think we can manage, yes—"

"Most commendable," he interrupted shortly. "I hope you *can* manage."

Clair bit her lip, annoyed with herself for her lack of diplomacy, but even more annoyed with Shane for taking offence so easily. Proud, arrogant man! Ever conscious of his own superiority simply because he was a highly prosperous farmer owning mile upon mile of forest in addition to vast citrus orchards and the lush arable lands adjoining those of Ngumi Farm.

"We shall try, Mr Neville," Clair assured him at length. "I expect, like all beginners, we shall learn by our mistakes."

"And lose by them," was his caustic rejoinder.

"But that's so like a woman," he added, just as if he had to, and a trace of humour lit his eyes as he saw Clair's chin come up.

"That," she said with fine dignity, "was a totally unnecessary remark."

"But one that appears to have made some impression."

"An extremely bad impression, Mr Neville."

For a long moment he regarded her in silence, and she was reminded of the times when Keith had told her she looked adorable when she was angry.

"Your flushed face and quivering lips, the way your lovely eyes flash – and even that frown has something inordinately attractive about it."

Disconcerted by her thoughts, she averted her head. Shane broke the silence at last, sending her completely off balance by asking her what she was thinking about.

"Your mind is a long way off," he added. "Perhaps you're back home, in England?"

"I was," she found herself answering, her thoughts still with Keith, whose face was clear, whose smile was tender. Tears gathered in her eyes, but she remained unaware of this, so absorbed had her reflections become. Keith. . . . He wanted her back. She had only to say the word and everything would be right again— But no ! How could she permanently exclude from her thoughts the miseries of the past ? – the humiliation and the hurt, suffered by her parents as well as herself ? Memory would surely force its way into her mind over and over again, no matter with what effort she commanded herself to forget.

"You have parents?" Shane's voice broke almost gently into her reflections and she glanced up, nodding as she did so.

"Yes, I have."

"They didn't mind your coming away like this?" he asked, and Clair attached no significance to the curiously perceptive glance he cast at her as he put the question. Her thoughts had wandered again and she saw the look of thankfulness on her parents' faces when she had agreed to come away with Jean and Sharon.

"They were *relieved* to have me come away—" Her voice clipped abruptly as she realized what she had said. She looked at him, hoping he had not fully absorbed her statement because if he had then surely he must consider it very strange indeed that she had used the word 'relieved' and in addition had actually emphasised it. His gaze was fixed and shrewd – and it was baffling, as was his action of slowly nodding his head as his face became thoughtful. He showed no surprise that she had cut her words, nor did he give the slightest indication that he would like her to continue. On the contrary, it seemed as if he actually understood why she had clipped her sentence like that – as if he knew the reason for her coming out here, to the lonely little farm in the northern Transvaal.

She stirred uneasily, bewildered by his manner. She would not have expected the superior Shane Neville to display the slightest interest in her, and yet undoubtedly he *was* interested in her.

"Shall we dance again?" he invited, but Clair shook her head. She wanted to be alone – out there in the darkness, detached from the gay crowd of dancers.

"If you don't mind – I'd rather not," she said. "I'm sorry. . . ."

Five minutes later she was outside in the gardens, walking slowly towards a shadowed building that looked like a thatched summer-house. All was silent except for the strains of the music drifting softly into the cool night air. As she lengthened the distance from the clubhouse the pulsing of cicadas became the predominant sound, and the darkness became more intense. With these changes came loneliness, deep and absolute. Clair felt utterly lost, filled with an all-pervading sense of hopelessness and despair. It had been a mistake, coming here tonight. And yet she had had no alternative, being forced to take over the driving of the station wagon. Had she refused to do so then neither of her friends could have attended the dance.

She continued to walk on, the air around her still humming with the sound of cicadas' wings rubbing together in the darkness. The drone of a beetle intruded, then the illusive cry of a solitary night bird. A pair of eyes glowed like embers as some nocturnal creature darted across her path, to dis-appear into the safety of the bushes. And still she wandered on, entering the small building almost without her own volition. Its inky blackness offered total isolation and she wanted nothing more. Groping about, she found what she expected to find – a seat running along one wall. She sat down, clasping her hands in front of her, aware of the strange, musty odour but not affected by it.

Keith. . . . His face again, and that tender smile. He had loved her dearly, but had become infatuated with another girl. Had he not gone to help his uncle it would never have happened. So why allow it to shatter both her life and his? He loved her still, had admitted his mistake and wanted her back. He had asked her forgiveness which, after all, was the limit of what he could do at this stage. He had promised to marry her at once – should she agree to return to him. He had promised to make her happy, to make amends for the misery he had caused her.

"Why don't I take the easy way out and go back?" she whispered on a great sigh which was almost a sob. "I love him still, and he loves me, so where's the sense in our both being unhappy?"

It was illogical for her to hold out like this, she went on to tell herself. Was she willing to live out her life alone, with a heart barren of love? This most certainly would be the case if she continued to allow into her consciousness the conviction that her memory would always prevail over her good intentions, that its ugly head would be forever there, even though she was making a desperate attempt to put from her those terrible days and weeks following that particular moment when the note was handed to her father and she knew instinctively that something

57

gravely wrong had occurred.

"I must try harder – and *harder*!" she cried in desperation. "I must forget! I *can* forget!" True, memory might intrude at first, but with the passing of time the hurt would subside and only happiness would prevail.

Yes, she decided, as she sat there in the darkness, she would go back. Her decision was firmly made; she would put an end once and for all to the doubts and uncertainty. She would be led by her heart and not by the cold logic which kept on sending out warning lights, telling her that marriage with Keith could not work out right.

Contentment settled miraculously upon her. Already she visualised the reunion. It would be bliss to have him hold her again, to feel his lips caressing hers. What of her parents, though? Clair knew without any doubt at all that they would not be pleased. On the contrary, she felt sure they would do everything in their power to dissuade her from marrying the man who had once jilted her. Her mother especially was bitter, and her father was angry, and would remain so. Would there be a rift? Clair frowned heavily, but was again soon thrusting away all doubts. Her parents loved her dearly and in consequence they would come round – if not at first then within a very short time.

"Sharon and Jean won't like it," she sighed, "but they'll accept my decision without any comment—" Clair's whispered words broke off, interrupted by the scream of pain that left her lips. "Oh . . . I've been bitten! It's – it's agony—" This time it was a gasp of pain that stemmed her words as, rising, she tried to put her weight on her left foot. Something had bitten her just above the ankle, and the pain was already spreading, with almost unbelievable speed and intensity, right up her leg.

Managing to take a few steps, she reached the door. Another few steps and she had the building behind her, vaguely wondering if it was a rat which had bitten her. Her leg was swelling fast and so were her hands; she was terrified, aware of an urgency and yet conscious of the fact that she was a long way from the clubhouse.

Another cry escaped her, echoing through lips that were stiff and cold, and she again tried to walk. If only she could manage to get as far as the lighted area around the clubhouse then someone would see her. But suddenly she fell forward on to her face, a little moan of pain and despair falling on the silence.

"Is anyone there?" Sharp the voice and demanding. Clair recognised it at once – and her terror was dissolved. "Is anyone there?" The repetition was still as sharp, but this time it came to Clair with less clarity. Her brain was becoming numbed and she called out quickly, fearing she would lose consciousness.

"Yes – pl-please help – me. . . ." The weak imploring tone ended with a gasp of sheer agony as Clair successfully stemmed the scream that strove for release.

"Miss Duncan!" Within seconds Clair felt herself

being lifted up, and it seemed as if her gesture, made in the darkness, conveyed to Shane the fact that she could not stand, for he changed his position at once and brought her into his arms. Carrying her as easily as if she had been a doll, he asked her what had happened. "You've fallen and sprained your ankle—" he was going on to say, when Clair interrupted him.

"I've been bitten by a rat – or something—"

"Bitten?" he snapped, his whole body stiffening. "Where were you?"

"In the summerhouse—" She broke off, gasping again. Shane was literally racing now, his long strides carrying him to the lighted lawn and across it, then down the side of the clubhouse to the side door. Stopping only to call out instructions that Sharon and Jean should come to the car park, he raced on. Reaching his car, he managed to open the door without putting Clair down. She was conscious of running feet, of exclamations and a babble of voices above which rose that of her cousin. The question Sharon asked was instantly cut short by the curt urgency of Shane's voice.

"Get into the back of the car and help me in with her!"

"Yes. . . ." The commotion was in full swing by this time; people were gathering around the car, and more and more running footsteps were heard. Then Jean's voice – a horrified exclamation issuing from her lips:

"Snakebite!" as she obeyed Shane's harshly rapped-out command for her to get into the passenger seat beside him. The drive, with no regard for speed limits or the ruts in the road; the hospital with its clinical smells, the stretcher and words drifting into Clair's fast fading consciousness, words like "snake venom" and "serum"—all was becoming more and more hazy to Clair. She did try to speak, but willingly gave up when Sharon gently urged her to be quiet.

"Hush, darling. Just relax."

Much later Shane Neville came to her bedside. Sharon and Jean were already there, both having been through a most anxious time while Clair was unconscious. She had now regained consciousness, but a terrible weakness held her in its grip, and her voice was slurred as she began to thank Shane for the prompt action which had saved her life. She did not manage to get very far in her expressions of gratitude, being interrupted by Shane, who told her that he had just been speaking to the doctor.

"You've to stay here until tomorrow," he continued, his critical grey eyes running over her drawn face. "I'll come for you about three o'clock."

"Thank you – for everything," she managed weakly. "I'd have died but for—"

"My car will be more comfortable than your station wagon," broke in Shane abruptly. "In any case, there doesn't seem to be anyone able to drive it at present."

"No." Clair moved on the pillow. Aware of Shane standing watching her, she was suddenly aware also of something provocatively baffling about his manner. It was almost as if he were examining her every feature for the first time – taking in the delicate contours of her face, the shape of her nose and mouth, the colour of her hair and eyes . . . even trying to probe beneath the exterior, as if assessing her character. She was embarrassed, unsure of herself, and she spoke in order to ease these feelings, saying again that she could have died, but this time it was Jean who interrupted her, hurriedly, as she noticed the frown of impatience which had appeared on Shane Neville's forehead.

"You'll be as right as ever in a few days' time, love. But for the present you're to take things easy, the nurse told me— Ah, here she is! I expect we've to go?" Jean looked at the nurse who had entered. "You're ordering us away?"

"I'm afraid so," smiled the nurse with a nod of her head. "The patient must rest now."

True to his promise Shane arrived the following afternoon to take Clair home. She was carried by him to the car, as the doctor had said she was unable to walk still. She knew she looked tired, with little lines around her eyes that seemed to have aged her ten years or more. For some reason which she did not even trouble to analyse Clair hated the idea of Shane seeing her looking so unattractive.

His eyes took it all in, but his face remained an inscrutable mask. However, as they drove from the hospital grounds he said,

"You'll not feel yourself for a week or more. Your stamina's low, which is only to be expected."

"You've had experience of snakebite before?"

"Of course."

"It happens often, then?"

Shane was shaking his head even before she had finished speaking.

"Not often at all. Snakes usually keep away from humans. But sometimes they'll nest in a shed or summerhouse – providing the building's been unused for some time, of course. You were just unlucky." Shane paused a moment and then, slanting her a glance, "Why were you there, all alone in the darkness? I'd asked you to dance again, if you remember? You chose to wander off all by yourself. It isn't natural." Something cryptic in his tone alerted her and she was reminded of that occasion when she had gained the rather absurd impression that he knew of her past. It was the same now; there was something strange both in his tone and in the silence which followed his words.

"You say I was unlucky." She spoke swiftly, desiring both to break the silence and to avoid answering his question as to why she had wandered off into the summerhouse. "On the contrary, I was most fortunate in that you happened to come along at that particular moment." She was leaning back, in the position in which Shane had placed her as he made her comfortable. A rug was wrapped around her legs even though the breeze drifting in through the open window was warm. "I've been told – by two people who were in hospital with me – that snakebite's a killer if it's not attended to immediately."

No comment from Shane. He was staring ahead,

to where a row of dome palms waved their spidery heads against a clear blue sky. He was driving alongside a thorn-bush hedge which skirted one long wall of the hospital grounds. Soon this was left behind, replaced by well-kept bungalows whose luxuriant gardens afforded a veritable tapestry of exotic colour, while the groves of trees between each bungalow gave a pleasant verdure and softness to the landscape.

"I can understand your disliking the idea of my thanking you," ventured Clair at length, "but I feel also that you should be understanding and realise just how deep my gratitude is."

Another silence, while she waited, sure he would make some sort of response, even though it might turn out to be one of abrupt impatience. However, there was not a trace of impatience in his tone when at last he said,

"You've already thanked me, Miss Duncan." He looked sideways at her, his manner one of impressive gravity. "As you've remarked, it was a fortunate circumstance that I happened to be close by when you cried out. I'd decided to take a stroll, in order to get some cool fresh air into my lungs." He twisted the wheel, avoiding a little furry creature that had come into the road in front of the car. "Will it satisfy you if I say that I do understand how deep your gratitude is?"

A swift smile broke over Clair's face.

"Yes, indeed it would!"

"Very well," he returned, a hint of humour in his

voice. "I've said it. And now can we forget all about it – the gratitude, I mean?"

She nodded.

"Yes, of course."

"Good. And now you'll perhaps answer my question?"

"Your question?" she prevaricated, turning her head away from him and staring through the side window at the area of hard-baked earth which had followed upon the last of the bungalow gardens. Under the intense heat of the sun the moisture quickly vanished from such regions and as the surface hardened so the vegetation withered. With the coming of the rains all would spring to life again, all would be green and pleasant.

"My question about your being alone in the summerhouse." Slight impatience edged his tone, but that was all.

"I wanted to think," she said briefly.

"About what?"

Clair kept her head turned away from him.

"You wouldn't be interested, Mr Neville."

"What makes you so sure?"

She turned then, to examine his profile. It was rigid, like the immobility of a statue carved in granite. There was nothing at all to be gathered from it, and yet she sensed an interest, knew the question had some meaning.

"I don't understand you," she murmured at last, and a light laugh escaped him.

"How like a woman to keep on prevaricating.

All right, Miss Duncan, you prefer not to talk, so we'll leave it at that. In any case, we haven't far to go. I hope you'll stay in bed for a day or two?"

"Yes, certainly I will."

"You always obey doctors' orders, then?"

"Not always," she confessed, relieved at the change of subject. "But this time I must. I should hate to be laid up for any length of time just because I didn't take care in the first place."

"Your conscience would prick you if you couldn't do your share of the work?"

"It wasn't that. . . ." She allowed her voice to trail away, wondering why she did so. She was going to tell Shane of her intention to leave Ngumi Farm and return to England, but for some reason she had changed her mind.

"No?" he was saying as he turned the car into a smaller road which would lead eventually to the rutted path off which lay the drive to Ngumi Farm. "What was it, then?"

She shrugged her shoulders.

"Nothing of importance."

"What an enigmatical person you are," he remarked, not without a tinge of amused sarcasm in his tone. "Do you always talk in riddles?"

"I'm sorry." Her voice was stiff suddenly, and cool.

"Don't apologise. I wasn't really curious, but merely making polite conversation – or rather, endeavouring to do so."

The sarcasm this time could not possibly go

undetected, and Clair coloured.

"You make me feel embarrassed, Mr Neville."

"Embarrassed?" he echoed in some surprise. "I can't see why."

"Well . . . I'm filled with gratitude for your saving my life, so I naturally feel awful if you act as if I've been ungracious to you."

"Ungracious because you avoid answering my questions?" She said nothing in answer to this and Shane went on, the familiar impatience entering his tones, "I said we'd forget all about the gratitude. Please don't mention it again."

Nothing more was said between them until, reaching the front door of Ngumi Farm, he brought the car to a standstill.

"We're here. Don't forget to rest."

The two girls came out, having been waiting for the car to arrive.

"The bed's ready, love," Jean told Clair, watching with an odd expression as Shane lifted Clair into his arms. "If you'll take her to the end of the passage," she added, following Shane into the house. "In there – yes, that's the room."

Sharon followed closely. Shane put Clair on to the bed and stood for a few seconds looking down at her. A smile fluttered to her lips.

"Thank you," she said simply. Shane inclined his head, turned to bid the other two girls good afternoon and then he was gone.

CHAPTER FOUR

CLAIR lay staring up at the ceiling of her bedroom, her mind confused by the indisputable fact that the cool urbane Mr Neville had some peculiar effect upon her. She thought of the times he had carried her – four times in all – and of the way she had derived comfort from the feel of his arms about her. The first occasion being when she was so ill after the bite, she could easily understand her feeling of comfort, simply because his very presence meant succour at a time when she had given up hope of anyone finding her, so far from the clubhouse. But what of those other occasions? Just a short while ago, when he had carried her into the house and into her room . . . the closeness of his body, the awareness of his cool clean breath as her head rested on his chest, the sudden shock of contact with his fingers as he put her down and she gripped his hand for support.

She tried to switch her mind to Keith – and found Shane Neville's image intruding, his clear-cut features, his proud mouth, the gravity of those steely grey eyes widely set beneath straight dark brows. So different in every aspect from Keith, who was shorter, lighter in colouring and far less arresting in the way he carried himself.

Clair thought of her decision to return to England,

and to Keith. She had it all cut and dried, out there in the seclusion of the summerhouse; she and Keith would marry at once, they would look for a home to replace the little house which had been given up. Yes, it was all so straightforward, once she had reached a definite decision ... but now. . . .

Although she managed to put Shane's image from her she could not bring into focus the picture of Keith and herself reunited. It was all too vague, unreal as a dream or a desire which cannot materialise.

She sighed, turned her head, then sat up and reached for the glass of lemonade which Sharon had put on the table by the bed. Sipping it, and with her pensive gaze fixed to the window where a feathery casuarina tree made gentle fluttering sounds on the glass as its foliage was swayed slightly in the breeze, she admitted that once again she was in a state of indecision. Perhaps the snakebite had been a blessing in disguise, preventing her from making the statement which would have informed Sharon and Jean of her intention to leave Ngumi and marry Keith. For had that statement been made Clair knew she would not have thought of going back on it. There would have been no reason for doing so because at that time she knew her own mind; it was Keith she really wanted to marry. Now, she was unsure of herself again – and all because of a man for whom she had no feelings other than the deep and profound one of gratitude.

White scuds of cloud passed behind the tree,

momentarily masking the intense blue of the African sky. From below the window came the sound of metal scraping on stone – Jean cleaning the lichen from the rockery stones, a task she had said was to be done in between the more important jobs.

"We must spend a little time on making the garden pretty," she had declared, and both Sharon and Clair had agreed. It would be nice to have lots of flowers as a setting for the homestead.

"How are you, pet?" Clair's musings were interrupted by the door opening and Sharon's soft voice putting the question. "Want anything?"

Clair shook her head, passing over the empty tumbler when her cousin held out a hand for it.

"No, thank you, Sharon."

"Tea'll be served at six or thereabouts," grinned Sharon, her grey eyes bright with humour. "How very nice to be sitting there, like a lady of leisure—"

"Oh, Sharon, don't!" implored Clair even though she fully appreciated that it was all in fun. "I feel terrible – a shirker!"

"Rubbish." Sharon was serious all at once. "Clair, my girl, you had us worried, I can tell you. If Shane Neville hadn't happened to be there—" She broke off, shuddering visibly. "I could never have faced your parents if anything had happened to you, since it was my idea that we come out here."

"Don't think about it. It didn't happen."

"No, but such an occurrence makes you think. Both Jean and I have been moving warily, and we've

70

decided to ask Mr Neville if he'll lend us a couple of his men so that our sheds can be examined."

"You don't mind asking him a favour like that?"

"It was Jean's idea, and I agreed with it. After all, he's our nearest neighbour——"

"But we said we'd not ask him for his help." Why was she taking this attitude? Clair asked herself in some bewilderment. From some remote place in her mind came the knowledge that she did not want Shane Neville coming to Ngumi Farm. But why?

"I know we did, but that was when we thought he wasn't nice to know."

"And now he is nice to know?"

Sharon's eyes opened very wide.

"He saved your life!" she exclaimed. "Of course he's nice to know!"

"I didn't mean it quite like that," returned Clair, looking a trifle distressed. "I'm filled with gratitude for what he did for me, but he's still the man whose opinion of women riled us at first."

"You sound as if you don't like him, despite what he did for you." Sharon moved, to place the tumbler on a table by the door. But her eyes never left Clair's face; she was puzzled and it showed. Clair bit her lip, unable to explain just how she felt.

"I don't dislike him," she began uncertainly. "On the other hand, I can't suddenly change my opinion of him simply because he saved my life. Gratitude I owe him, and respect in consequence. But it's not possible for me to find him attractive. He's cynical, for one thing – look at the way he spoke of our sex!"

"Oh, nonsense," returned Sharon lightly. "We took the wrong attitude right from the first."

Clare shrugged her shoulders.

"It's clear that both you and Jean have changed your minds about him."

"We have, and it's natural. I don't understand you, Clair. He's put himself out today in fetching you home from the hospital and yet you can be like this—" Sharon stopped speaking as perception dawned. "Of course! You're a man-hater now, it would seem. Well, that's a depressing way to be, and an illogical one as well. Hate Keith by all means – I'm sure I do! – but for heaven's sake don't go about hating every other man too."

Faintly Clare smiled, but it was not a happy smile.

"I've aroused that temper of yours and I'm sorry. Please count me as nothing when you and Jean are making decisions where Shane Neville is concerned. If he comes around I shall be charming to him, but my emotions might not match my manners."

Sharon sighed and picked up the tumbler.

"I'll bring you another drink," she said, and went out.

The following day Shane Neville called and was shown up to Clair's room.

"It's at his request," explained Sharon hurriedly, having run to the room in advance of Jean who was conducting him there after she and he had been chatting on the stoep. "He asked if he could see you."

Clair frowned and her eyes flashed towards the mirror on the dressing-table. Her hair would be untidy, for she had been sleeping until a few minutes ago; her eyes would probably be dull— What did it matter? Who was Shane Neville that she should care about his opinion of her?

He came in and Sharon left, saying she would have coffee ready in about ten minutes' time.

"Thank you," he returned graciously, the merest of smiles touching his mouth. "And how are you feeling?" he asked, turning to Clair.

"Much better, thank you."

"You're not so drawn," he stated, his eyes critically examining her face. "I'm glad to see you resting. I had visions of you getting up and doing some work."

"I said I wouldn't disobey the doctor's orders," she reminded him.

"Women have a habit of changing their minds."

"Their prerogative, it's said."

"A sign of irresponsibility."

"Aren't men ever irresponsible?"

"They might be, sometimes. The only man I knew who was irresponsible was old Mr Lumley."

"And he ought to have been a female." This was out before Clair had time to think, and Shane raised his eyebrows interrogatingly.

"What gave you that idea?" he demanded shortly.

She bit her lip, then decided that an honest answer could do no harm.

"You once said it, I believe?"

A small silence ensued before he said,

"So he passed it on to his niece?"

"His great-niece, yes."

Amusement entered Shane's grey eyes.

"What else did he pass on?"

Clair looked at him, and drew in her breath. He was too handsome by far, and too noble in his bearing. She looked away, unaccountable anger welling up within her.

She did *not want* to be conscious of his attractions!

Because of her anger she forgot to be tactful.

"You said he was obstinate and meddlesome, and that's why he ought to have been a female. You also implied that females are lacking in both sense and wit." There, it was all out, but she suddenly wished it had been kept back, for Shane's mouth had set in a grim line, and his eyes narrowed to pinpoints of bright metal.

"Perhaps I should have added something about their good manners," he said icily.

Clair said nothing; she could not find anything to say. She felt guilty, remembering what she owed to him.

"I'm sorry," she murmured at length. "I ought not to have been so outspoken."

He looked down at her, frowning in thought.

"You have a grudge against men, haven't you?" His words were so unexpected that she jumped, and sent him a startled glance.

"Why do you suggest a thing like that?" she asked.

"It isn't very difficult to sense."

She bit her lip, drawing it tightly over her lower teeth.

"It isn't just you," she found herself saying.

"I did put my sex in the plural," he reminded her. He had moved and was standing with his back to the window. Behind him, the casuarina tree tossed its foliage against the backcloth of a sunlit sky.

"Yes, you did." She paused a moment. "You were right," she added then. "About my having a grudge, I mean."

His eyes narrowed again.

"Someone at home?" he queried.

"I'd rather not discuss it."

"Just answer this one question. Is the grudge as strong as it was — against the man who caused it?"

She sent him another startled glance, then suddenly stiffened as enlightenment penetrated into her brain.

"You found my letter," she stated, and Shane instantly nodded his head.

"I make no apologies for reading it. It was torn and dirty when one of my men brought it to me. I began to read it, which was natural. And as I had no idea to whom it was addressed I continued to the end. Then it dawned on me that it might belong to one of you girls. I discovered which one when I heard your name: Clair."

"At the dance." She was blushing hotly as she recalled what was contained in the letter. "Your reading my letter explains several things which have puzzled me," she managed after swallowing several times to remove the tightness in her throat.

"Not least of which is my question about your having a grudge against men," he said.

"I'm not a man-hater, if that's what you think."

"But you've no intention of allowing yourself to fall in love again?"

"That's right." She was still blushing, and desired nothing more than that he should leave her.

"You didn't answer my question: is the grudge against the one who jilted you as strong as it was when you first came here?"

She looked bewilderedly at him, forgetting her embarrassment. For there seemed no need for it; Shane was speaking as if he were conducting some sort of cold and clinical investigation.

"Why should you be interested – one way or the other?" she queried, a curious edge to her tone.

Shane ignored this.

"As you've still not answered my question, I take it that the grudge has lessened?"

She found herself nodding in agreement.

"I still love him," she said simply.

It seemed that Shane gave an impatient sigh. But it was something more than impatience that she caught in his voice. It was undoubtedly concern.

"You're not thinking of trying to mend what has been broken, I hope?"

"Going back to him, you mean?" The situation was becoming more and more baffling, since she failed utterly to understand why he should be concerned about her.

"That's what I mean. He asked you to go back, swore he'd made a tragic mistake in jilting you at the altar—"

"Oh, *please*!" she broke in, distressed. "Have you no consideration for my feelings?"

"Not if you are going to make certainties out of doubts—" He paused, noticing her puzzlement. "You should know what I mean by that," he told her sternly. "You've been going over and over it all in your mind, asking yourself if it would work—" He stopped and his gaze could only be described as a glowering one. "Haven't you?" he added authoritatively, and Clair found herself quite unable to offer him a protest, much less an open denial.

"Well, yes, I have."

"And your conclusion?" His voice was taut, his eyes still glowering and hard.

"I was intending going back."

Silence, long and profound . . . and fraught with suppressed anger on Shane's part. Clair felt it, deep and intense. What was the matter with him? Why this strange reaction? It mattered not at all to him whether or not she left Ngumi Farm and went to England to marry Keith.

"When are you going back?" The question came at last, spoken in imperious, vibrating tones.

"I said I *was* intending to go back."

He looked swiftly at her.

"You've changed your mind?"

"I can't say. It was in the summerhouse that I made up my mind to return to Keith. Then the snakebite. . . ."

He was nodding and she trailed off.

"So that was why you went away, to be alone in the dark." Again he nodded, mechanically. "Perhaps you can now see what I meant when I talked about your making certainties out of doubts?"

She nodded and said quietly,

"Yes, I do." A small pause and then, thoughtfully, "I expect I did make certainties from doubts."

His grey eyes softened a little. She knew he was satisfied by her admission.

"Did you know that it's also possible to make doubts out of certainties?" he queried unexpectedly.

Her eyes flickered uncomprehendingly.

"What do you mean by that?"

"Certainties can stare you in the face, but you can't even see, much less believe."

She frowned at this and said impatiently,

"You accused me of talking in riddles, but you're doing the same!"

A little more softness entered his eyes, and a hint of amusement too.

"I admit it, Clair. And I won't explain, so the riddle stays a riddle." He changed the subject, telling her that she and her friends were invited to a barbecue at the Club President's house.

"I saw his wife, Elsie, in town this morning. She

sent her apologies for not being able to visit you while you're laid up, and asked me to tell you about the barbecue. It's a week on Saturday, so you'll be feeling quite fit by then."

"That'll be nice." She felt shy, because he had called her Clair, and she lowered her eyes. Shadows lay on her cheeks as the sun through the window lengthened her already long and curling eyelashes. Unconsciously, she allowed a smile to hover on her lips, a tremulous smile of the kind which had brought from Keith, so many times, the assertion that he wanted to kiss her over and over again, just for the pleasure of seeing her lips tremble in this particular way. "If you see Mrs Fowler please convey my thanks for the invitation."

"I'm afraid I shan't be seeing her. She's going away for a week, visiting some relatives in Pretoria. That's why she isn't able to visit you. You'll be having one or two other visitors, though," he added. "They'll bring you books and fruit and the like." He stopped speaking as he heard Sharon's voice. She was calling out to tell him the coffee was ready. "Think well before deciding your future," he said swiftly, watching Clair's face with an odd expression as she raised her lashes, revealing those violet eyes in all their limpid glory. A muscle pulsated in his throat; he said abruptly, "And when your decision *is* finally made, come and let me know what it is."

"Let *you* know?" She stared at him. "Is it of so much interest to you, Mr Neville?"

"Shane's the name. I myself have already dropped

the formalities, but perhaps you didn't notice?"

"I did . . . yes."

His lips twitched.

"You're shy. How refreshing!" He turned to the door. "Yes, it is of so much interest to me," was his final sentence before he went out, closing the door quietly behind him.

Clair stared at the door for a long time, wondering at his words. It was of interest to him to learn of her decision. . . .

"He can't *care* for me," she whispered. "So what is his reason for being interested?"

The answer came later in the afternoon. Marie Kellar called, bringing two books and a glossy magazine which was a current copy and had never been opened. She brought a basket of fruit which had obviously been made up by an expert, but whether it was Marie or not Clair never found out, as her visitor talked incessantly, barely affording Clair an opportunity of saying much more than an odd yes or no.

But when she had gone Clair said to Jean, who had entered the bedroom with the tea-tray,

"I've just learned that Shane Neville's sister was jilted at the altar."

"She—!" Jean stared disbelievingly, the tray poised over the bedside table. "But how incredible! Where is this sister now."

"Living in England. She married an English businessman just over a year ago."

"Not the man who jilted her?"

"No – she had married him previously. They never made a hit of it and were divorced within two years of the marriage."

"Marie Kellar told you all this?" Jean put the tray down and removed the cosy from the small brown teapot.

"Yes." A pause ensued while Clair hesitated, undecided about revealing what was in her mind. However, she spoke eventually, and Jean listened, the changing expressions of her face requiring no words to explain them. "And so," ended Clair, "Shane's interest in me is explained. He doesn't want me to make the same mistake as his sister made."

Jean was nodding thoughtfully.

"It's decent of him to take this interest."

"I suppose it is." Clair's voice was flat, expressionless. She could not have explained her feelings; all she knew was that a strange dejection had come upon her when she had realised just why Shane Neville was so concerned about her. His concern was impersonal, the natural instinct of any thoughtful person to steer another away from disaster.

"Imagine him reading that letter—" Jean stopped, and spread a deprecating hand. "Sorry, Clair. I'm the world's most undiplomatic idiot!"

"You're nothing of the kind! It doesn't seem to matter that he read it. I was embarrassed at first, but it very soon passed and we discussed the matter just as I've explained to you."

"I think it's jolly decent of him to want to protect you," declared Jean, repeating something of what she had said before. "You've not yet made up your mind, you said?"

Another hesitation, and then,

"At present, I haven't. I did, though, just before the snake bit me. After that it all seemed different and I was right back where I started – not able to make up my mind."

Jean looked at her, mechanically twisting the knitted tea-cosy in her fingers.

"Shane obviously doesn't think you could make a success of marriage to a man who could be as callous as Keith. Sharon and I are in agreement, Clair. You can't go back to Keith!"

Clair gave a small sigh.

"Sometimes life is more than bearable, it's pleasant. Keith's image scarcely ever intrudes, so I'm free as regards memories. But at other times I can't get him out of my mind no matter how I try. If he hadn't sent me that letter I'm sure I'd have managed to get over it in time, but the knowledge that he loves me—" She stopped and shook her head, a brightness entering her lovely eyes. "It seems so illogical for us to be apart when we love each other so much."

"You still love him?"

"Of course. . . ." Clair's voice trailed away and she frowned. For it was not Keith's face she saw in her mental vision, but that of Shane Neville.

"You're quite sure?" There was an odd inflection in Jean's voice and her eyes were fixed searchingly upon her friend's face.

"Of course I'm sure."

But Clair turned away, unable to meet that piercing gaze.

"Well, you might be sure," was Jean's dry rejoinder, "but I'm not. If you ask me, you've almost got that cad right out of your hair."

CHAPTER FIVE

As time passed Clair dwelt again and again on Jean's firm assertion that she, Clair, had almost got Keith out of her hair. It was difficult to disagree with Jean, but equally difficult to accept the fact that her love for Keith had not been nearly as strong as she had believed it to be. For surely, if it had been strong, she could not stop loving him as quickly as Jean was implying.

"Well, love, this is your last day in bed. Tomorrow you're allowed up!" Sharon was smiling down at her cousin. "My, but I'm happy to see you looking so well!"

"Tell me about Shane and the cows he's getting for us." Clair was sitting up, a book open on the coverlet in front of her. "Jean's mentioned that he has a plan whereby we can have cattle on the hire purchase?"

"That's correct. We mentioned it to Bill and he says he ought to have thought about it. It appears that some farmers breed cattle to sell to those who are less prosperous. They pay for them out of the money they get for the milk – and the products they make from the milk, of course."

"That's wonderful! You can't lose, can you?"

"Only if a cow dies. You still have to pay for it. However, Shane's seeing that we're fully insured against such an eventuality."

"He's good to us," murmured Clair pensively. "And just to think, we were going to show him he was right when he said women were obstinate and contankerous – and the rest."

"I know," with a grimace. "I was ready to be his sworn enemy." Sharon paused a moment. "Do you like him any better now?"

Clair looked at her, and nodded unconsciously.

"Jean's told you everything, of course? You know about his reading my letter from Keith?"

"She said you'd told her you didn't mind her passing it all on to me."

"That's true. I've no secrets now – not from anyone around here," Clair added, her eyes straying to the smaller of the two windows. Shane Neville's homestead could not be seen from the window, but the large wooded region in which it nestled formed an entrancing part of the view from that particular side of the house.

"He's pretty astute, that one. Just look at the way he's glimpsed all our difficulties. He didn't hesitate to lend us those men to examine our sheds, as you know, but we hadn't asked for help to repair that old stove. Shane noticed the smoke bellowing from the chimney and immediately sent a couple of his men to put it right."

"He's proving to be a very helpful neighbour."

"He was rather sarcastic about our method of growing tomatoes, though," said Sharon, laughing.

"Those on the rubbish tip, you mean?"

"Yes. He happened to see them when he went to examine the state of our barn. He's bringing us some plants, in pots which you can put straight into the ground. He has this special strain which he maintains, will produce three or four times the quantity as those we have."

Shane called later in the day, bringing the plants and the insurance forms, these latter to be filled in by Jean and returned to him. He came up to Clair's bedroom, preceded by Sharon who left a moment afterwards, saying she would make some coffee, which he could have with her and Jean on the stoep before he left. Clair, having heard him arrive in his car, had leapt out of bed and brushed her hair. It was not exactly at its best as it required a wash, but it shone for all that. She used the blusher, and applied a little colour to her lips. And then she realised she did not require any artificial colour on her cheeks after all. They were reddening of their own accord, because of what she was doing – making herself attractive in case Shane should come up for a word or two with her. She stood, regarding her face in the mirror, the idea of self-analysis foremost in her mind but ruthlessly driven out by the vision of a white-clad bride, waiting in a crowded church while the futile moments dragged by, each one longer than the one before it. Not for her another experience like that, nor even the risk of it.

Why was she thinking on lines like this? Shane Neville's interest in her had been explained by the fact that his own sister had suffered a similar hurt and humiliation; he was anxious that his neighbour should not make the mistake which his sister had subsequently made, hence his demand – for it had certainly been a demand – that Clair should tell him, when eventually she made her decision.

Her decision. . . . When she was sitting there in the summerhouse, in the darkness and the silence, she had made the firm decision of returning to Keith, of marrying him and attempting to forget that past hurt. Then the snakebite and the timely appearance of Shane. The hospital and what took place afterwards. All this was upsetting, but there was no reason why it should have affected her decision. Clair recalled how comforted she had felt once she had made up her mind to marry Keith. All the doubts and uncertainty had dissolved and she could see only happiness.

But Shane had told her that she had deliberately created certainties from her doubts, and she had agreed with him – after she had thought about it, that was.

How very easy to sway one's mind, inclining it to accept what was not really there.

"I don't love Keith. . . ." Wonderment mingled with disbelief brought an added depth to her violet eyes – and it was at this moment that Shane appeared, tapping gently on the bedroom door and actually opening it without waiting for her invitation to enter. She swung around, blushing to the roots of her hair as she saw his eyes wander from her face to her breasts, revealed partly by the low V-shaped neckline of her flimsy, transparent nightgown. Every curve of her body could be seen through it.

"Oh. . . ." That was all she could find to say. And she could not move, her legs refused to carry her back to the bed.

"I'm sorry. I didn't expect you to be out of bed." So cool the tone, with no depth to the actual apology. It was almost as if it were a natural thing for him to see her like this. "Can I pass you this wrap?" He had it in his hand, a "happi-coat" which she had bought from a friend who had purchased it in Hong Kong. It was of vivid turquoise, with exquisite quilting in gold and silver thread. The collar was high, of mandarin styling.

"Thank you," she stammered, holding out her hand for it. "I – I didn't expect y-you to come in like that."

She was looking down at the floor; he held on to the wrap and she glanced up, questioningly.

"Turn around," he ordered, but she shook her head.

"No – I—" Shane turned her around and put the wrap about her shoulders. "I w-want my arms in it," Clair said peevishly. "The material's slippery; it'll fall off my shoulders." Anger was rising at his action. She had resented being forced to turn around; she felt he had done it only so that he could see *more* of her figure.

"Very well." The coat was taken from her and held out. Clair put her arms in it and began to fasten the buttons.

"I don't understand you," she said, still in the same peevish tone of voice.

Shane laughed; Clair caught her breath, all her anger dissolving. What an attractive man he was! How had he managed to remain a bachelor so long? He must be at least thirty, she thought, seeing in her mind's eye the several lovely girls who had been at the Club dance. Not one of them had made eyes at him, or gone out of her way to hold his attention. No, they already knew it was no use, decided Clair. Shane Neville was not interested in women. They were obstinate and cantankerous; they possessed neither nous or wit.

"So you don't understand me, eh?" he was saying, his eyes continuing to wander over her in spite of the protective covering she had donned. "Remember what I said about its being possible to make doubts out of certainties?"

She stared at him, puzzled.

"Well?"

"Think about it some time." He changed the subject with an abruptness that was startling. "I merely came over to see Jean about the insurance, bringing her some forms to fill in, so I haven't much time. I wanted to see how you were, that's all." He paused a moment, noting the hand she had put to her cheek. She was still aware of her heightened colour, and her hand provided a welcome coolness. "You'll do," he added. "Sharon tells me you're getting up tomorrow."

"That's right. The doctor dropped in to take a look

at me – that was yesterday. He was quite satisfied with my condition." Clair was speaking in a low tone, her mind so confused that she could scarcely think. All she knew was that a quiver of disappointment had passed through her when Shane said that he was not staying.

"Don't think you can begin working right away." Shane looked sternly at her. "You're not up to it yet."

"No, I realise that." He was moving towards the half open door; she watched the easy swing of his tall body, and the confusion of her mind increased. No doubt about it, this man was beginning to have a profound effect upon her emotions.

The room seemed empty when he had gone – not merely empty, but desolate, she thought, then gave herself a mental shake.

"I don't want to like him!" This was not the first time she had uttered such words, but never had they been uttered with such vehemence and strength. "No, I don't want to like him – and I *won't* like him!"

Yet she found him continually intruding into her mind, and now she was no longer attempting to superimpose Keith's face. Keith no longer mattered. She had lost all she ever felt for him and she was elated in consequence. No more hurt, no mind-switching from one decision to another. She would have to write him a letter, though, informing him that she no longer loved him.

But the following afternoon, when she was sitting

on the warm but shady back stoep, Bill arrived, bringing with him the mail, which he had thoughtfully collected when he was in town. Clair took the letter calmly – much more calmly than the first one she had received from Keith. Sharon and Jean, who had come along on seeing Bill's car arriving, both glanced at the handwriting.

"A letter from Keith," said Sharon in an expressionless tone.

"Here's another for you – and two for Jean. Sharon, nobody loves you except me." Bill smiled at her; the three girls stared at him, none of them able to interpret that last phrase.

"It's from my parents." Clair fingered the second envelope lovingly. They wrote regularly, desiring to know how she was feeling. In her answer this time she would have good news for them. They would learn with relief that she was no longer in love with Keith. She would make no mention of the snakebite, Clair decided. It would only make them apprehensive that the same thing might happen again.

"Well, how about this for a piece of news?" Jean, having opened one of her letters, waved it in the air. "Do you remember my friend Christal Warrender?" Jean was speaking to Sharon. "We lost touch when she went to live with her rich aunt in Spain—"

"The glamorous one," broke in Sharon, nodding her head. "Yes, I remember her. Full of confidence and beautiful as a dream. She's written to you?" added Sharon, glancing at the letter with a puzzled frown.

"She's not only written, but she wants to come over for a holiday. She learned of my inheritance here from an old office colleague of mine. This colleague passed on the address and Christal decided to write. Apparently the aunt died and Christal's now one of the idle rich."

"Are you going to let her come?"

"I think so." Jean glanced from Sharon to Clair, and then to Bill. "You'll fall for her," she laughed, "but so will every other male around here. Christal's dynamite, but choosy. Hence the fact that she's still a spinster. What say you two—?" Jean transferred her gaze. "Shall we invite her to be our guest?"

"It's all right with me," said Clair.

"And me. It'll be a change, having another girl here. How old is she?"

"Oh . . . let me see. . . ." Jean pursed her lips in thought. "Around twenty-eight, I should think."

"What makes you say I'll fall for her?" Bill wanted to know, his eyes wandering towards Sharon.

"All the men do – and always will do while she looks the way she does."

"What about her disposition?"

"Nice, but I must admit she can be catty at times—" Jean gave a shrug of her wide bony shoulders. "But can't every female, if and when it becomes necessary?"

They all laughed. Then Bill began talking about the poultry at Ngumi, advising that another strain of hens should be introduced. Clair excused herself and went to her room. But once again she felt caged, and she decided to venture as far as the little shady bower in the garden. It was away from the stoep, affording complete privacy.

Keith's letter was opened first – another entreaty, and asking why she had not written, answering his first letter. He repeated his statement that he would remain a bachelor all his life if Clair decided against marrying him.

"I love you with all my heart," read Clair, turning over the page. "What made me do such a terrible thing to you I can't imagine. It makes me shudder to think about it now. Our little house has been let only temporarily, to a couple who've come here to work for six months. We can have it back, Clair, and I still have all the things I bought. We'll soon make it what it was, a pretty little nest for two. Then we shall build later, a large house in its own grounds, with a swimming-pool and tennis court—"

Clair lowered the paper, feeling almost nauseated by its contents. Bribery. . . . This was what was being offered to her.

"What do I care for a big house with a swimming-pool!" The letter was screwed up into a tiny ball and held in her hand. "It happens to be love I want – which you say you have for me, I know. But I do happen to want reliability, fidelity." Clair slipped the ball of paper into her pocket. The other letter was opened and a smile fluttered to her lips. The same dear familiar opening: "Our beloved

93

daughter". Then the same anxious inquiry.

"Are you well, love? Are you happy? Time is passing, and soon you'll be able to laugh again." And so it went on, with items of local news following. But then Clair's eyes began to sparkle and she read the passage a second time. "And now for the final item before we close. Father and I are coming over to see you. Yes, Clair dearest, you're not seeing things. Your father never gambles, as you know, but a man who was new to the firm had some lottery tickets of some kind which he was selling for charity. Well, need I explain? Yes, your father won the first prize, which was a thousand pounds. We didn't need to ponder on what we would do with the money. So, darling, we'll be with you in about a month's time, when all arrangements have been made. Luckily, Dad didn't take his full holiday last year, so he has an extra week owing to him. His boss has been generous and given him another extra week, making five in all. If Jean can't put us up we'll stay at a small hotel in town. Let me know, dear, and if your house isn't large enough for us will you please make enquiries at once and let us have details as to prices? No more for now. Our dearest love to you, as always." Both her parents had signed it, and both had added four kisses.

"Oh, but this is marvellous news!" Clair held the letter to her heart, and there was never a thought for the one rolled up, in her pocket. But she did think, later as she made her way back to the stoep, that fate had been more than obliging when it kept her from writing to Keith. Yes, the snakebite had been a blessing in disguise and no mistake, since, had she written to Keith, she would now be on her way home and her parents would have been robbed of their trip to Africa.

Reaching the stoep, she sat down. Sharon had made a pot of tea and she instantly began to pour a cup for her cousin. But she stopped, the pot in mid-air, and stared into Clair's eyes.

"You're – very – happy," she faltered, lowering the pot without pouring out the tea. She glanced at Jean, whose gaze was also fixed on Clair's radiant face. Jean merely nodded, while Bill, naturally puzzled by all this silent by-play, and aware that something of unusual importance was going to be mentioned, quaffed the last of his tea and rose at once. Clair, faintly puzzled by Sharon's manner, suddenly realized what she was thinking. And Jean too. They had both concluded that her glowing look was the result of something contained in her former fiancé's letter.

"Yes, I'm happy," she said swiftly. "Mum and Dad are coming over for a visit."

Silence. Bill broke it with a cough.

"I'll be going," he said.

"Okay," from Jean, whose relief could be felt. "We'll see you at this barbecue, I expect?"

"Of course." He said goodbye and was gone. Sharon had poured the tea and Clair was helping herself to sugar.

"I thought at first that it was Keith," began

Sharon. "For one awful moment my heart sank right down into my feet."

"I'm sorry. I didn't realise I looked so delirious," added Clair ruefully. "Father won a prize in a lottery – the first prize of a thousand pounds." Clair went on to say what else was in the letter; when she had finished Jean and Sharon spoke together.

"They must stay here. We'll make room somehow."

The last sentence came from Jean, whose brow was already creased in thought.

"Your friend's coming as well," Clair reminded her. "We've only one spare bedroom."

"Two of us could share," said Sharon without hesitation. "The only problem is beds. We need a double and a single."

"It'll be expensive to buy them," said Clair, troubled. "I think I must make inquiries in town—"

"No such thing!" broke in Jean emphatically. "Your mum and dad are more important than Christal, who's only coming for pleasure, anyway. Your parents are coming to see you – and they're staying here!"

And so it was agreed that Sharon and Clair shared a bedroom. Jean's room was very small – she had insisted on taking the least attractive of the bedrooms despite indignant protests from her two partners – and so it was impossible for Christal to share with her, as there was room for one single bed only. Clair's room was also small but large enough to take a double bed.

"I'll buy a *kaross* when I'm in town," decided Clair excitedly. "Then Mum can take it home when she goes."

"One of those lovely fur rugs made from the skins of dassies and other animals," inserted Sharon. "Yes, that would be nice for them to use and then to take away as a souvenir. We'll also buy a new lamp for beside the bed; yours is just about on its last legs, Clair. I noticed that it doesn't always stand up straight."

Clair laughed. She was happy, and excited. She said after a while, glancing from one friend to the other, "If I show you Keith's letter you won't require any further explanation of how I now feel about him." She withdrew the ball of paper as she spoke, and held it on the palm of her hand. "He's offering me – at some future date, mind – a large house with a swimming-pool and tennis court—" Clair frowned and shrugged and put the letter back into her pocket. "I was disgusted. I'll throw this in the stove when I go into the kitchen."

"It really is all over, then?" from Sharon, and her indrawn breath of relief could be heard. "You were so sure you still loved him that I was afraid you'd just have to go back."

Jean was drinking her tea, and regarding Clair from over the rim of the cup. Meeting her rather amused gaze, Clair smiled and said,

"Yes, Jean, you were right when you said I didn't love him."

"I'm glad you found out before you'd made a

mistake, though."

"So am I?" rejoined Clair with a shudder. "How dreadful it would have been had we married!"

"And then found out you couldn't get along. Oh, well, for those that do make such mistakes there's always the divorce court." But there was no lightness in Jean's tone. She had always maintained that prevention was better than cure. She was also old-fashioned about marriage, believing that people should make sure – should even live together before marriage if there was any doubt at all in either of their minds. Clair's parents were also old-fashioned about marriage, neither being very happy when Clair's aunt and uncle decided to get a divorce.

"Are you not writing to Keith, telling him of your decision?" inquired Sharon with interest.

"I will do, yes. It'll be a very short note, though."

She was in town, taking the letters to be posted, when she literally bumped into Shane. She had been loitering, looking out for a *kaross*, when, turning quickly from a stall, she came face to face with Shane, whose arms came out and grasped her elbows.

"I do wish women would think before they act! A man would stop to think that there might be someone behind him!"

Clair stared in dismay, believing at first that he really was annoyed. But suddenly a smile broke over his handsome features, and a hint of amusement entered his eyes. His hands remained on her elbows;

she was intensely aware of them, and of his bodily closeness. She looked up and her face was very near his chin. His eyes held hers and she quivered mentally, her soft lips parted in a tremulous half-smile.

"I'm . . . sorry. I was clumsy, I'll admit—"

"Did that fellow Keith ever tell you how pretty you were when your lips trembled like this?"

"Yes—" Clair stared up at him, confused and self-conscious. She had no cool confidence, like his, no easy manner of assurance. She was like a schoolgirl – gauche, embarrassed.

"Then *I* shall tell you you're adorable." And before she had time even to lower her head his lips came down and met hers.

"Oh," she quavered, stepping back, "you shouldn't—"

"Why shouldn't I kiss you if I want to?"

Clair shook her head in a gesture of bewilderment.

"I've never been able to understand you," she complained. "Why are you so interested in me? Is it because of—" She stopped, having almost mentioned his sister. He might not like the idea of the gossip, she suddenly thought, and added quickly, "Because you're sorry for me?"

Shane's grey eyes flickered.

"I rather think you'd resent my pity, Clair."

She nodded mechanically.

"I'd hate it," she owned.

"Come and have some refreshments with me," he invited. "If you've shopping to do then do it later.

99

Did you come to town in the station wagon?"

"Yes. I felt like a drive, since I've been confined to the house for several days."

They were walking along, under an avenue of eucalyptus, while stretching away in the distance was the apparently endless succession of undulating countryside where tall grasses waved and palms looked black against the sky.

"Our small town must seem very lacking in comparison to your sophisticated London stores." Shane looked down as he spoke, noting the sunlight in her russet hair; it brought out lights that looked to him like pure gold, copper-tinged. "Don't you ever lose patience with the inadequacy of this place?"

Clair was swift to shake her head.

"I love it! I love everything here," she added without thinking, and in came her companion with,

"Including me?" and he laughed as the colour rose in her cheeks.

"Don't be silly!" She looked away, acutely conscious of increased heartbeats and racing pulse. "My parents are coming out to see me," she said in a determined effort to veer him totally into another channel. "I've just sent them a letter saying how delighted I am."

"Your parents?" he echoed with interest. "That'll be nice both for you and for them." They reached the teashop, and Shane took Clair's arm in the most proprietorial manner and conducted her through the bougainvillaea-framed doorway into the dim and shady courtyard beyond.

"This table, sir." A waiter was already holding out a chair for Clair to take. "I'll bring the menu."

She said curiously,

"Your men speak of you as 'baas', and I've also heard the native waiters use the same expression. But this man called you sir."

"Baas means master. I am not this man's master, so why should he address me as if I were?" Shane seemed faintly annoyed and Clair lowered her head, feeling she had been reprimanded.

"I was only curious," she murmured apologetically, wondering why she should suddenly have lost her buoyancy, simply because Shane seemed displeased with her. She had never been so troubled about Keith's reaction to anything she said. Keith. How remote he was! It seemed impossible that she had ever been engaged to him, much less on the point of marriage.

"Tell me more about this visit of your parents," invited Shane when the order had been given and the waiter had gone to fetch their tea and cakes. "When are they to be expected?"

"In about a month. I shall be hearing soon about the flight."

"How are you going to bring them from the airport?"

"The station wagon," she answered, but even as she began to think about its inefficiencies Shane was offering to bring her parents in his car.

"Your vehicle could break down on a long journey

like that," he went on. "Besides, your parents will be more comfortable in a car."

"It's awfully kind of you, Mr Neville—" She broke off, because of the raising of his eyebrows and because she knew what he was going to say to her.

"I believe I asked you to call me Shane."

"Yes. . . ."

"Perhaps you don't care for it? I have another – Robert," he added, amusement glinting in his eyes. "Would you prefer this very English-sounding name?"

"No, I like – like – Shane. . . ."

"And now we've surmounted that little obstacle, we'll talk about this visit. But first—" He stopped, considering her thoughtfully, examining her features, her eyes. "Have you reached a decision yet regarding this Keith?"

A small silence ensued before Clair spoke.

"I've decided to stay here."

Another silence and then,

"A most wise decision. Clair. I'm relieved for you; it would never have worked."

She looked at him across the table, looked into a face of severity and into eyes that had gone hard and brittle. She could not resist saying,

"You sound so sure that it would never have worked."

"I am sure." Clair waited expectantly, hoping he would mention his sister. It was not that she felt any idle curiosity, but naturally she was interested, as it was a strange coincidence that she should meet, and get to know, someone who was related to a girl who had suffered a similar hurt and humiliation to that which Clair herself had suffered. But Shane spoke again of her parents' visit, this time asking how the girls were going to put them up.

Clair explained, adding with a wry grimace,

"It'll be a bit of a squash for everyone. The rooms at Ngumi are all so small."

Shane made no comment; his brows were drawn together in a thoughtful frown.

"I have plenty of room," he said at last. "They're very welcome to sleep at Watsonia Lodge."

Watsonia Lodge. . . . Although Clair had not yet been inside Shane's white colonial mansion, she had seen it several times from the outside. Flower-bedecked – with many glorious blooms climbing up impressive stone pillars – it stood in elegant seclusion on a small rise, surrounded by exotic gardens embellished by statuary and fountains, and with a wider circle of mature oak and cedar trees. A veritable palace for her parents to stay as guests of Shane.

"I don't know what to say," she told him. "You overwhelm me with such a kind offer."

Shane's fine lips twitched.

"You never expected your neighbour to be so accommodating?"

She had to laugh then, and said,

"We all decided to have the game, seeing that we'd the name. We intended being obstinate if and when you might offer suggestions as to the running of our farm. We said we'd act as if we'd neither wit nor sense."

His laugh rang out, and Clair's mingled with it.

"Mr Lumley must have been particularly trying that day, for I assure you, my dear, that I'm not normally so ill-mannered or critical."

"But you did compare Mr Lumley with my sex," she reminded him a little tartly. "We concluded that you hadn't much time for women."

At this he looked hard at her.

"I didn't, I must admit."

Didn't. . . . What did that mean? Clair's pulse raced again, and she was thankful for the chair beneath her – because her legs were suddenly feeling rather shaky.

"We have another visitor coming," she told Shane. "A friend of Jean's. I think Jean was seriously considering putting her off, or making her stay at the hotel here. This was after Jean was told of my parents' projected visit. However, Christal will now be able to come. We'll have a houseful," she added happily. "It'll be fun, cooking for them and bringing them into town for the odd meal."

"We shall have to put on a little entertainment," he decided. And then, curiously, "Christal? That's a glamorous sort of name. It conjures up a golden blonde with a sylph-like figure and the face of an angel." He was laughing with his eyes, but Clair was grave all at once. She suddenly wished Christal was not coming. . . . But how silly, and how selfish. Jean would be delighted that her friend could be put up at Ngumi Farm, after all. "You haven't yet said whether or not you're going to accept my offer," Shane was reminding her as the waiter appeared with the tray.

"But of course I'm accepting, on their behalf. And thank you very much, Shane. It'll save us some money, too, because we'd have had to buy a bed for them. We'll only have to buy one now – a single for Jean's friend."

"We'll see about that later. I can either put the girl up or lend you a bed."

"I'm sure Jean would prefer Christal to stay at Ngumi. But she'll be grateful for the bed."

CHAPTER SIX

THE tea was served and Clair poured out, her whole mind on the words she had just uttered. Why had she been so quick to declare that Jean would prefer Christal to stay at Ngumi? It would be far simpler for the girl to stay at Shane's home; there would then be no necessity to decorate the spare room, or to find furniture for it, from other rooms. And what of Jean's wishes? She might jump at the chance of having her wealthy friend sleep in a luxury home rather than the small, poorly-furnished room that Ngumi had to offer.

"What are you thinking?" demanded Shane, breaking into Clair's reverie. "You're frowning a little, so it isn't altogether a pleasant matter which occupies your mind."

She put down the teapot, and handed Shane his cup and saucer. She had to be honest, so she told him that perhaps she should have left the decision regarding Christal to Jean.

"Jean might prefer to accept your offer," she added, in her imagination seeing the glamorous Christal reclining with poise and well-assured ease on some large, damask-covered chair in Shane's elegant sitting-room.

"I'll put it to her," decided Shane, and then, after he had taken a drink of his tea, "Tell me, Clair, do you feel happy now that you've decided to stay here?"

"Yes, I do."

"You intend staying for a long time?"

"I can't say. If I feel the wrench acutely when my parents leave again I might reconsider, and go home." She paused a moment. "But I shall never have anything to do with Keith."

"When I asked if you intended staying for a long time I suppose I was really trying to find out if you'd be able to settle here."

"Settle?" Clair wished he would not say things like this. For her confused mind could not grapple with their exact meaning. Settle. . . . It was a strange thing to say— But no, it was not strange at all. It was natural, seeing that she and her friends were now farmers. And the question was merely put because of interest, and not for any other reason.

Shane Neville was not considering marriage to her.

The shock of this mental statement shook Clair to the very marrow. Where on earth had such an idea come from? He had shown interest, true – but she now knew the reason for that interest, and it had nothing personal about it at all. He had kissed her, but did that mean anything these days? There had been no passion in the kiss, no desire. It was light and swift. It was the kiss a man might give to his sister – certainly not to the girl he hoped to marry.

What else was there to account for that statement she had made just now? Nothing – just nothing.

"I'm a fool," she said to herself. "In any case, I've vowed never to let any man do that to me again."

She could never imagine Shane jilting a woman at the altar, but then she had never imagined Keith doing so, either. Men were so unpredictable; you could never be sure of their intentions – or their actions.

He was speaking again and she gave him her attention. He spoke of the cattle they were having; he mentioned the crops, saying he would lend the girls some of his employees.

"Later, you'll be able to employ help of your own," he continued. "You certainly need a house-boy. Women don't slog away in the kitchen here."

She looked swiftly at him.

"You don't believe, then, that woman's work is in the home?"

"Certainly not!"

His vehemence surprising her, she said,

"You would want your wife to be a lady of leisure?"

"I would want her to spend some time on herself – on her appearance." He stopped and a touch of amusement had entered his voice when he continued, "I'd expect her to be so attractive that I'd want to kiss her every time I came into the house."

Clair blushed, although she could not explain why.

"A glamorous girl will be your ultimate choice, then?"

He looked hard at her.

"I expect that, like every other man, I have an eye for beauty."

"We were speaking of glamour."

"*You* were speaking of glamour," he corrected.

"Well – you didn't answer my question," she persisted, a challenging expression in her violet eyes.

"Glamour's a strange thing," he admitted, surprisingly. "At times it can be attractive, while at others it can pall."

"Depending on both the man and woman?"

Shane nodded in agreement.

"My mother was glamorous," he explained. "She was beautiful and my father worshipped her."

Idly Clair chose a cake and put it on her plate. This situation was intimate; it seemed to be bringing her close to Shane. She did not want to be close . . . or did she?

Confusion again, and the subsequent warning that, in any case, Shane was not for her.

"Your father evidently liked glamour," she said, and Shane nodded, his eyes again settling on Clair's face in an examining way.

"He did. And it was not only in Mother. He always had an eye for a glamorous woman; it was a great disappointment to him that my sister was the homely type."

"Your sister?" Clair stopped a moment, and picked up her cake fork. "She's – married, isn't she?"

"You know about her?"

She told him of Marie's visit to Ngumi. Shane

nodded, requiring no further explanation.

"I thought you'd be annoyed at the – well, the gossip," said Clair, looking a little anxiously at him. His mouth was tight, but that was all.

"Everyone knows about the disaster of Avice's first marriage. Marie obviously told you everything."

"Yes; it seemed a very strange coincidence that I should meet someone who had experience of being jilted at the altar. . . ." Shane was actually smiling and she added swiftly, "You know what I mean!"

"Yes, my dear, I do know what you mean."

My dear. . . . The second time he had said that. It meant nothing. Clair did not want it to have any significance whatsoever!

"Tell me more about your mother," she said. And then, "I believe Marie mentioned that both your parents were dead?"

"They are." He spoke calmly; Clair did not feel the need to say anything sympathetic to him and she merely waited, while he spent a few moments in thought. That he was in the past was clear, and when at length he spoke it was to mention several incidents of his childhood. Clair learnt that there had been another child, a girl, who had died at the age of three years. Avice was two years younger than Shane, and between the two there existed a close, but carefree, relationship. "We don't see very much of one another," he went on. "I shall probably have a trip to England in the not too distant future."

"You know England?"

"I've been a couple of times, that's all." Shane

changed the subject, reverting to the subject of his mother. "She combined beauty, glamour and a sort of severe nobility with the charming qualities of understanding, compassion, and love. She loved deeply – her husband and her children. We were a remarkably happy family."

Clair looked at him across the table. He was staring vacantly in front of him, absorbed in memories, and so she had the opportunity of examining his every fine line and feature. It was clear from where he had acquired that air of severe nobility, those inordinately handsome features. But did he possess the finer qualities of which he had spoken? Had his mother passed on to him understanding, compassion, and the ability to love deeply? Something caught at Clair's heartstrings. She suddenly knew he could love with a depth that would release those less fine qualities – passion and primitive desire. The girl whom he eventually married would experience love in all its primeval forms; she would be brought to complete surrender by the strength of her husband's passionate lovemaking.

Colouring at these thoughts and pictures, Clair lowered her head, concentrating on the delicious pastry which lay on her plate.

"It's time we were moving." Shane spoke some time later, sending Clair a smile as he did so. He had spoken about his parents all the time, telling Clair how and when the Boers had come to settle here. They had wandered away from their British rulers to stake claims on the eastern plateau.

"It was a wilderness, but they desired solitude – in fact, my ancestors had a passion for it. Hence the lonely locations of the homesteads, so far-flung from one another, as you will already have noticed."

"I too love the solitude," Clair had told him, and he had seemed pleased at her statement, casting her a strange look . . . an almost tender look. And now, as he waited for her to gather up her handbag and her cardigan, he was sending her a similar glance. One of her tremulous smiles fluttered and she saw his eyes widen. He opened his mouth to speak, then closed it again. Clair felt a sense of loss, subconsciously wishing he had voiced the words which had plainly risen to his lips.

As they went along the street he asked her what she wanted in the way of shopping.

"If you do it I can then carry it back to the station wagon for you," he added.

"Mainly I came to send off the two letters," she told him. "But I was intending to buy a *kaross* for my parents' bedroom. I thought they could take it back, as a souvenir."

"I think you'd better leave it, seeing that there's no urgency now. You might like to take your parents on a trip to Pretoria while they're here, and they'll have much more choice there."

"A good idea," agreed Clair. "In that case, I haven't much to get – just a few groceries and a tube of toothpaste for Jean."

An hour and a half later she was back home. Her face was flushed, her eyes sparkling. Unaware of these attractions, she was taken aback when Sharon in a dry voice asked her the reason for them.

"You've just mentioned that you had tea with Shane — so it might be that the answer to my question lies in that direction?"

"I don't know what you mean?" But her increased colour gave the lie to this.

"Then don't bother answering me." Sharon and Jean exchanged glances. Jean said slowly, and in a voice that sounded distinctly flat,

"Shane seems to like you enormously, Clair."

Swiftly she shook her head, remembering her slight suspicion that Jean was attracted by Shane.

"We're friends, that's all."

"You talked, in the café?"

"Yes, he told me about his parents, and his sister."

"About all his family, in fact. Hmmm. Significant."

"Don't be silly," frowned Clair. "Shane would never look at me in that way—"

"It would appear that he already has, my love." Jean managed a thin smile. "Good luck to you, Clair. You deserve someone nice after what you've been through." And with this Jean rose, took up the tube of toothpaste which Clair had placed on the table, and left the room.

Deeply troubled, Clair looked at her cousin.

"She likes him, I knew it. But why she should suspect Shane of being interested in me I don't know — what I mean is, Sharon, he wouldn't be interested in a personal way."

"I thought, once, that his interest was merely that of an anxious neighbour who wanted to help someone make a right decision. But not now, Clair—"

"Oh, for goodness' sake, Sharon! I've told you – Shane is not interested in me in *that* particular way!"

"All right," frowned Sharon. "There's no need to be shirty about it." She paused momentarily, her eyes once again taking in her cousin's appearance. "You yourself – can you honestly say you're not falling for him?"

Clair stared at her, anger in her gaze.

"No, I am not falling for him! You know very well, Sharon, that I have no intention of ever falling in love again as long as I live! What kind of a fool do you take me for? One jilting's enough for me; I'm not taking any risks of the same thing happening again."

"Be logical! The chances of a repetition are a million to one!"

"They can be ten million to one as far as I'm concerned! I've said, I don't intend taking any chances, and I mean it."

Despite these emphatic declarations Clair, on her own in the privacy of her room, had to face the fact that was staring her in the face. She was not only deeply affected by Shane, she was very close to becoming involved in emotions which she would prefer to leave dormant for the rest of her life. Love was not for her, and in any case, what was more unprofitable than falling in love with a man who wanted glamour in his wife? Shane had not said so in actual words, but the fact stood out, revealed both by his descriptions of the woman who would eventually appeal to him, and by the attitude of his father. He had been attracted by glamour, so it was reasonable to assume that his son would also be attracted by it – more especially as his mother was so glamorous.

After a wash in the earthenware bowl on her marble-topped dressing-stand, and a change of dress, Clair brushed her hair and went along to the sitting-room. It was empty and she turned to the kitchen where she began to prepare the vegetables that lay on the draining-board, having been picked from the garden only a short while ago. Jean came in as Clair was engaged on this task and the two exchanged smiles.

"Are you up to this?" Jean wanted to know. "You've been out, remember, and that's tiring in itself."

"I feel fine, Jean. Don't worry any more about me." She put a peeled potato on the board and began to cut it into slices. "Shane's offered to have Mum and Dad at his house, just for sleeping, of course."

"He has?" blinked Jean, and then her lashes fell, hiding her expression. As she saw this, Clair experienced a sense of discomfort, for it was plain that Jean was again attaching significance to something which Shane had done. "Well, that's most obliging of him, I must say. You accepted, of course?"

"I did. It's solved a major problem. He also said that your friend could stay there. Alternatively, he's willing to lend us a bed."

"You did have a long and intimate discourse together, didn't you?"

"Jean . . . please don't infer anything. You know very well that I'm not interested in falling in love again – now or at any other time."

"You know I like him, obviously. My own fault; I gave it away. Well, he'd never have looked at a straight up-and-down female like me anyway."

An uneasy silence fell between the two girls, broken at last by Clair, who again brought up the question of accommodating Jean's friend Christal.

"I told Shane that I thought you'd prefer to have Christal stay here, at Ngumi—"

"You did? Why?" Jean's voice was sharper than ever Clair had noticed before. "The decision is mine, surely?"

"Yes, most certainly it is. So I told Shane he had better see you."

"But you've just admitted to getting Christal accommodated here."

"You didn't allow me to finish," Clair pointed out, trying to keep her patience. "I was going on to say that, after thinking about it, I'd told Shane to see you."

"I feel that Watsonia Lodge is a much more fitting place for Christal to stay than here, at Ngumi. She's used to a luxurious bedroom and it's unlikely she'll be one hundred per cent happy and comfortable in our tiny spare closet."

"No. . . ." Again the picture of the glamorous Christal reclining in one of Shane's armchairs. . . . "Well, he's seeing you quite soon, so you can tell him you're accepting his offer."

Jean nodded, then frowned and looked hard at her friend. For no reason at all Clair was reminded of Jean's assertion that all women can be catty if the occasion called for it – or words to that effect. Clair dismissed the recollection with all speed. Jean would never do a thing like that – throw her glamorous friend at Shane just to remove his interest from Clair – the interest to which Jean was attaching far too much importance anyway. But how could Clair make this clear to her? Looking at Jean's face now, and seeing the dullness in her eyes, Clair felt a spasm of pain shoot through her. Jean was suffering; no doubt about that.

"I must go out and help Sharon with the weeding." Jean turned, without looking at Clair, and left the kitchen through the back door, which she left open. Clair's distressed gaze remained on her back until she was out of sight.

"Perhaps I shall go home, after all," said Clair to herself. "It certainly would solve all problems. Jean would feel better and so would I. . . ." But would she herself feel better? Not to see Shane again – ever. Not to talk with him, and walk with him. Never to feel his arms around her because they would never attend another Club dance, never to see his smile, a smile that undeniably sent pleasant ripples along her spine. Why was the man so devastatingly attractive? It wasn't fair to her sex! No man should be able to affect a woman in the way Shane could affect them. But perhaps his particular type of attraction did not attract all women. Would they attract Christal, the girl who had not yet married, because she was far too choosy – so Jean had declared. Christal was rich, too, and she had glamour and poise. Thinking about it, it seemed almost impossible for Shane and Christal not to get together —Clair's musings came to an abrupt end as she heard Bill's cheery voice calling from the stoep,

"Hallo, is anyone about?"

"I'm here." Taking up a towel, Clair dried her hands. "Do you want Jean?"

"I want you," he told her softly. "I thought I might find you alone, in the house. Is there anywhere where we can talk?"

"I don't understand, Bill. Why should you want to talk to me – me particularly, I mean?"

"You'll soon understand," he assured her, glancing towards the open door with the sort of furtiveness one would connect with some kind of secrecy. "Where can we talk undisturbed?"

"Here, I suppose. Sharon and Jean are weeding. It rained last night, as you know, and—"

"Can we go to your bedroom?"

Clair's eyes opened very wide.

"What on earth for? And supposing the others come in and find us there? No, you'll have to talk here, Bill, I'm sorry."

"All right," resignedly. "If they do come we'll have to change the subject." A pause. He delayed speaking for so long that Clair broke into his indecision and asked outright what he had come for.

"It's important, obviously," she added, "so it's surely not all that difficult to broach."

"It's Sharon," he said briefly.

"Sharon?" Clair stared perceptively at him. "So you weren't joking the other day when you said you loved her?"

"I wasn't joking." He was calm, but colour had crept beneath his tan. "What I want to know is: do you think I have a chance?"

"Wouldn't it be better to ask Sharon herself?" rejoined Clair reasonably.

"I'm so damnably shy when I'm with her alone!"

"That's not unnatural, if you're in love with her. But you'll have to speak to her some time, so why not now?"

"I'd like to have something to go on. Has she ever talked about me?"

"We've all talked about you, Bill, because you've been so good to us, such a great help. And Sandy too, even though he's not so sociable as you are." She paused, puzzled by his reluctance to approach her cousin direct. "You'd be far better to approach Sharon, Bill. She can only refuse you—"

"I couldn't bear it!" he cried. "No, I want to discover her feelings first, Clair."

"Then why not – er – court her?" she suggested,

finding something quite amusing in a man like Bill lacking the courage to ask a woman to marry him. "It is usual, you know."

"I can't get anywhere near her! She seems not to have noticed that I care for her."

"You could easily make her notice."

"How?"

"By the ordinary methods—" She broke off, spreading her hands in a helpless gesture. "I'm not a man, so I haven't any idea of how a man's mind works."

"I love her, and that's about as much as I can tell you. I've never had anything to do with girls before and so I haven't any experience. If I had just one little clue, I'd manage to pluck up some courage and ask her to marry me. But as things are I feel she thinks no more about me than those damned chickens out there!"

Clair had to laugh, and she continued to do so in face of his glowering stare.

"I'll tell you what," she said at length. "I'll try to find something out—"

"Don't ask her if she loves me. Just try to pump her."

"I wouldn't dream of asking her if she loves you. But I will try to find out if she has any affection at all for you."

"Thanks— Here she is! I'll say I've come about the tickets for the next Club dance."

CHAPTER SEVEN

It was two days later that Clair said, very casually,

"You've been teasing me enough about Shane, but what about Bill . . . and you?"

Sharon turned from the sink, and stared blankly at her cousin.

"What on earth are you talking about?"

"Bill seems to be inordinately interested in you—"

"Not me particularly," broke in Sharon, and Clair, deliberately keeping a close watch on her expression, could not fail to notice the faint tinge of colour that stained her cheeks. "He's interested in the farm – which means us all, the three of us."

Clair shrugged, adopting a careless manner.

"If you think so, Sharon. For myself I feel he's more interested in you than either Jean or me." She turned, to dry a large baking bowl which Sharon had placed on the table, since there was no room for it on the draining-board. "He's nice," she murmured, pushing the cloth into the bowl.

"I agree; he's nice."

"But you're not attracted to him?"

"Look, what is all this?" demanded Sharon. "Are you having a joke with me, or something?"

"No, I'm not. I'm just asking you a simple question."

"Then here's a simple answer: no, I'm not attracted to Bill!"

Clair picked up a cup from the draining-board, while Sharon went back to her washing-up. After a long and not very friendly silence Sharon muttered, rather sulkily,

"I'm sorry I lost my temper."

"That's all right. Forget all about it."

Another silence, broken only by the clatter of dishes being washed and placed on the draining-board.

"It isn't as if Bill's ever made any approaches. I can't think what made you ask questions like that."

"Supposing he did make any approaches?"

Sharon turned.

"You're persistent, aren't you? There must be a reason."

"There is. I'm of the opinion that there's some attraction between you and Bill. I might be wrong," Clair thought to add carelessly. "If so, then I'm sorry. I was seeing things that didn't exist – drawing wrong conclusions."

Sharon wiped her hands on her apron, and as she looked at her Clair saw again that tinge of colour in her cheeks. Also she deliberately avoided Clair's eyes as she said,

"Bill's far too occupied with his farm. He has no time for falling in love."

"I wouldn't be so sure. Most men fall in love some time."

"I've no time either," stated Sharon, just as if

Clair had not spoken at all.

"Everyone should have time for love, Sharon," said Clair gently.

"What about you? You say you'll never fall in love again as long as you live."

"I did have time once," she reminded her cousin, still adopting that gentle manner. "In my case there's an excuse for not wanting to fall in love."

"Bill has Sandy to think about. He couldn't take a wife home—"

"Certainly he could. They're partners. Besides, Sandy's very fond of you, so he'd be delighted at the idea of your living there."

"You really think so—?" Abruptly Sharon broke off, eyeing her cousin accusingly. "You trapped me into admitting that I – er – like Bill!" she almost snapped.

"If you like him then why don't you let him see it? I have a feeling that Bill is the kind of young man who would require some sign before he made a proposal of marriage."

"I'm going outside," said Sharon pettishly. And she went, leaving a smiling Clair behind her, a huge pile of dishes waiting to be dried.

"Well, at least one of us is going to find perfect happiness," said Clair in a satisfied little voice. And she began to hum a little tune to herself as, turning, she continued with her chores of drying the dishes.

The barbecue was held on a wide lawn shaded at its

borders by tall palms and oaks. Native women were at the fires, cooking chicken legs and sausages and other appetizing meats. Clair was with Jean, waiting for their meat, while a little distance away Sharon and Bill were talking as they ate their food. Lights in the trees gave the atmosphere a romantic quality; there was laughter and chatter and soft music which could be heard only now and then above the other sounds. Sandy, who was far more reserved than Bill – but who was later to prove far less shy – came over and chatted for a while. He was still with them when Shane approached, having arrived late owing to the failure of the electricity in his house.

"We couldn't find the fault," he said, "but eventually we succeeded." He glanced around. "The same crowd," he smiled. "Clair, can I take you over there, to where the cutlets are being cooked?"

"We were waiting for the sausages," she began, but Shane interrupted her, in the most imperious and proprietorial manner, saying she would enjoy the cutlets far more than the sausages.

"Also, they're better for you," he added. "More protein."

Clair looked at Jean and hesitated.

"Don't mind me," said Jean shortly. "Have your cutlets by all means."

Clair bit her lip, still hesitating. Shane took her arm and her mind was made up for her as she was led away, towards another fire, that glowed under the trees.

"I didn't like leaving Jean alone, Shane," she

protested, though a little weakly, since these was nothing she would enjoy more than to be with Shane, in the romantic surroundings of the Fowler homestead.

"She isn't alone; Sandy's with her."

"He'll not stay with her, though."

"Then she'll find someone else to talk to. Heaven knows, there are plenty of people here tonight." He paused and glanced down at her. "What's wrong? Don't you want to be alone with me?"

"Yes – no! Oh, I have to be diplomatic, don't I?" she said, flustered but determined to appear cool and composed. Too many times this man had disconcerted her; she was determined not to have him do so this evening. "I like your company. Does that satisfy you?"

"No, it doesn't!" And before she knew it Shane had swung her right off her feet and was carrying her towards a little copse, lonely and dark. "And now," he said, "I shall kiss you as I mean to kiss you in the future!"

"No, you will do no such thing—"

But he did, and with force. Her mouth was forced open under the pressure of his. She gasped inwardly, fighting for breath, but he was merciless.

"There, my little one! You know just what you're in for!"

She swayed when he released her, and grabbed at the lapel of his white linen coat, drawing in great gulps of air and releasing them again. Her chest was rising and falling, and her mouth felt bruised and sore. She found herself recalling her previous conviction that Shane could display a primitive passion when making love. She had not been mistaken!

"You're – hateful!" she managed at last. "It wasn't as if I've ever given you any encouragement!"

"That's just it! I wanted to find out if you are really the block of ice you appear to be."

"I hope you discovered that I am!"

"Ah. . . ." He took hold of her again; she tried to free herself, but was hurt for her trouble, Shane proceeding to give her a good shake which, being so unexpected, resulted in her teeth coming together on to her tongue. Fury blazed within her, but it found no outlet as her lips were ruthlessly claimed again. "So you're sending out a challenge, eh?" he said, finishing the sentence he had been about to phrase when he decided to kiss her instead. "Well, my little one, we shall see. You're completely at my mercy here—"

"I could call out!"

"You could, but you won't. You'd only make a fool of yourself."

She glared up into his face, scarcely able to see it in the dark.

"You're despicable!"

"As I was saying," he resumed, calmly ignoring her wrathful words, "you're completely at my mercy here. I shall not allow you to escape until I've made you return my kisses."

"Then we shall be here all night!"

"Fine. That'll suit me, Clair. I'm sure we can find plenty to occupy our time."

"You're a cad!"

"But an attractive one," he said with a laugh. "You do find me attractive, Clair, it's just that you won't admit it – or have you admitted it, to yourself?" He held her from him, roughly tilting her face when she continued to look down at the ground. "I do believe you have, for I feel your body trembling. It's because you're so angry at my perceptiveness. To return to what I was saying just now – I'm intending to keep you here until I have some response from these beautiful lips of yours, lips that were meant to be kissed. I shall melt the iceberg and seek the fire beneath." His head bent; she tried to escape his demanding mouth, but it was a futile attempt. He was too strong for her puny efforts to have any effect at all, and she gave up, standing close and eventually being forced to lean against him as he insistently brought her even closer still. Every nerve was affected; she was on fire inside, but still she resisted, refusing to respond. And then, so unexpectedly that she gasped, his hand slid her shoulder strap down and cupped one small firm breast within its gentle warmth. She struggled, but only for a moment. The touch of his hand was sheer ecstasy, bliss that she had never experienced before. She succumbed, responding to his passionate kisses, to the sensuous movements of his body. His lips left her mouth and took the breast, so gently and with something akin to reverence. She lay passive against him, desiring only that this moment would go on and on . . . into eternity, where she and Shane would both float, locked in each other's arms.

"So. . . ." Satisfied at last, Shane released her, gently replacing her shoulder strap. "I succeeded, my love. And now there remains only the question, doesn't there? Will you marry me, Clair?"

She gasped. Never had she expected this – and so suddenly. True, he had shown interest, as she had admitted long before now, but she had believed his interest to be impersonal. Instead, everything he had done had been to one end – this.

"I can't marry you, Shane." Simple words, but firmly stated. "I've vowed never to fall in love again—"

"You *are* in love, idiot!"

"I'm not joking, Shane. I was never more serious in my life. I shall never run that sort of risk again."

"Risk?" he ejaculated, stunned by her implication. "My God, girl, you don't consider me that much of a cad, surely!"

"I didn't believe that Keith was that sort of a cad."

So cool her voice, so steady and firm. Shane looked down into her face, endeavouring to read it. But the trees spread darkness and, after a moment's hesitation, he took her hand and led her into the light shining from one of the trees nearer to the fire.

"You mean it?" he said, dazed. "Clair, I know you've been fighting this – I'm not obtuse by any means. Yes, you've been fighting, but after that little scene just now you have to admit to loving me. It was a callous method I adopted in order to prove to myself that you cared, but that is over now. We begin, we show each other our love, we become engaged, then married. It's inevitable, Clair; you can't escape your fate – yours and mine."

"It's no use. I shan't marry you."

"By God, but you will!" he returned harshly. "Do you think I would lose you, knowing as I do that you care? No, girl! You'll marry me if I have to take you away to some secret place to do it!"

"That's not sensible talk. You could never force me to marry you against my will."

"I could and I will—!" He broke off as Jean and Sandy approached. Jean stared into her friend's flushed face, saw the heaving bosom, the clenched fists, the trembling mouth. "We're just going to have some more cutlets." Shane's voice, urbane and controlled. "Perhaps you'll join us at that little table over there?"

"We'd be delighted," dryly from Jean, whose eyes were still observing her friend. "Were your cutlets as tasty as they smelled?" she added in a rather acid-sweet tone.

"Try some for yourself," Shane invited. "That will be the better test."

"Your taste might not be mine, eh?" remarked Jean, and then, to Clair, "You look rather hot. I must admit, it's a warm and sultry evening. Not the most ideal for fires and cooking. I expect you and Shane were near the fire?" she added, and suddenly Clair's eyes glinted, and she found herself saying,

"Does it matter whether we were by the fire or not? What's the purpose of such silly talk?"

"Clair!" admonished Shane, pretending to be shocked. "That wasn't very nice of you." His tone now held amusement, and his eyes twinkled. That scene might never have been enacted, those bitingly furious words might never have left those smiling lips.

"I'm sorry," she said, and received an approving nod from Shane for her efforts.

The rest of the evening dragged unbearably, since all Clair wanted was to leave the barbecue and return to Ngumi, and the peace and privacy of her room. She had been shaken by the events, torn by her own desires, hurt by Shane's anger. This, she thought, was almost as bad as that dreadful time when she had stood in the church . . . waiting for the bridegroom who never came. Emotionally it was as bad, but of course there would be no aftermath, no heartache and humiliation. Shane's threats meant nothing. He had been so angry by her refusal that he had said anything that had come into his head. Even now he was probably regretting his words; by tomorrow morning he would have made up his mind to forget her, write her off as one of his rare failures.

One idea emerged from all the others: she must now go home; there was no alternative, for she and

Shane could not possibly go on meeting one another. It would be too awkward for both of them. How relieved he would be when she told him of her decision.

This she did later, just as he was saying good night to her in the drive where she had left the station wagon. There was no sign of Sharon or Jean and Shane found Clair alone, standing by the vehicle, waiting for her friends to appear.

"Going home?" he repeated when she had spoken to him of her intentions. "Are you out of your mind?"

"I'm in a most rational state of mind, Shane," she assured him quietly.

"You're crazy!"

"Because I refuse to take another risk?"

"There isn't any risk! Look, I'll marry you next week – just as soon as I can get a licence. There'll be no time for changing minds – not that there's any likelihood of such a possibility on either of our parts. We're in love, Clair, deeply, madly, irrevocably in love, and you can fight it if you will, but you'll surrender at length."

She shook her head. But she did wonder how she could remain firm, when she loved him so – for she did love him, had been aware of it, in her subconscious, for some time now. He would not let her down; she was sure of it, and yet. . . .

"I don't want to be engaged to you—"

"Then don't be engaged, darling. Be married. I'll still buy you an engagement ring, because I know you'll want one to wear with your wedding ring, but as for any lengthy engagement – well, we'll dispense with the engagement, which, I can assure you, dearest, wouldn't have been a long one anyway. I want you, need you, as I've never wanted and needed a woman in my life. You're my all, Clair—"

"Please stop! Why can't you accept my answer? I don't want to marry you!"

"You will marry me!"

"Here's Sharon. I'll say good night, Shane."

He turned from her without a word, striding away to where his own car was standing.

"Guess what?" Sharon was saying excitedly, quite unaware that any little drama had been played out between Shane and Clair. "Bill and I are engaged!"

"Congratulations. How did it happen so quickly?"

"I did as you advised and gave him a hint that I was not totally cold towards him. If you missed us we were kissing and cuddling among those trees over there." She pointed to a clump of trees on the opposite side of the lawn to those in which Clair and Shane had been. "Oh, but I'm happy! Bill wants to be married within the month!"

"Our guest will be here, and Mother and Father."

"That'll be nice. Everyone likes a wedding. Clair love, I'm delirious!"

"I can see that," returned Clair a little dryly.

"Where on earth is Jean—? Oh, here she comes. We can go at last.

"I'm engaged to Bill," said Sharon as soon as Jean reached them. "We're getting married in about a month's time!"

"Congratulations. I'm not too surprised because I saw you go into that clump of trees over there. I also saw you come out. You looked very happy indeed."

"Shall we go?" Clair looked at Jean. "Do you want to drive? Your injury's better, so if you want to take the wheel—"

"I don't." The three girls got in and Clair started the engine. "What about you?" said Jean as the vehicle began to move. "Are you engaged too?"

"Clair!" gasped Sharon. "But—"

"I'm not engaged, nor am I likely to be." Taut the voice, but scarcely audible above the sound of the engine.

"When you came out of your little hideaway you looked as if you'd been made love to – violently!"

"Jean!" Sharon turned a pair of shocked eyes towards her. "What a thing to say!"

"Either they'd made love or they'd quarrelled," declared Jean tightly.

"We'd quarrelled." Clair decided it was best to tell them all – well, not *quite* all. But she did say that Shane had proposed to her – she had to, because this was her excuse for going home, her reason for leaving the farm which she had come to love. "I shall probably return to England when my parents leave," she told them finally. Jean said nothing, but Sharon protested, declaring there to be no sense in leaving when she wanted to stay.

"You and Shane will get over your quarrel," she stated. "I'm sure that neither of you are the kind of people to bear a grudge."

"I can't stay, so there's no more to be said." Clair put her foot down; the station wagon's speed increased.

The drive home was done in total silence from then on, but on their arrival at Ngumi Jean turned to her partners and told them of her intention of selling the farm to Shane.

"He wanted to buy it before, so I expect he'll buy it now. As soon as you've both left I shall be getting ready to leave myself."

"But what will you do, Jean?" Clair was distressed, and this was revealed in her voice. "You've put everything into this place. We've got it nice and cosy and almost making a profit. You can't leave it now," ended Clair persuasively, but Jean was already shaking her head.

"I can't manage it alone."

"You can get help – a couple of farm workers."

"I'm selling it," returned Jean and, turning on her heel, she left the room.

CHAPTER EIGHT

WHAT a muddle! And her parents coming to stay! Clair decided to arrange for them to stay at the hotel, as she could not now have them stay with Shane. He might not want them, anyway, not after all that had happened on the night of the barbecue.

"I'm going out this afternoon," she told Sharon as they all three sat at breakfast. "Is there anything you want?" Clair did not address Jean, because they had not been speaking to one another for over a week. It had not been Clair's choice and several times she had attempted to close the rift, but her efforts were futile. Jean was morose, and accusing. Both Clair and Sharon could understand, and commiserate with her. But both agreed that Jean's was a defeatist attitude, that she could keep the farm if she so wished. Shane would help her, that was certain. And until she could afford her own workmen he would lend her some of his, especially at harvest time, and when the weeds sprang up in their thousands after the rains.

"Not that I can think of at the moment," answered Sharon. "I shall have to go into town myself tomorrow, to try on my dress."

"That dressmaker's been quick, getting it cut out and ready for a fitting in so short a time."

"She's marvellous. If you'd been staying you'd

have had to go to her. All the people round here have their clothes made by her."

Breakfast over, Clair went off to see to the hens – to collect what eggs there were and to clean out the nest-boxes and line them with clean straw. Then she had weeding to do, and some work on the garden, for it had been agreed that the place must be kept in good condition so that Jean would be able to ask a decent price for it.

By one o'clock Jean had the lunch on the table. To Clair's surprise she spoke to her, asking if she would bring her back some notepaper.

"I have several letters to write," she added.

"You can have as much as you want of mine," offered Clair eagerly, so glad to be on speaking terms with her friend again. "There are plenty of envelopes as well."

"Thanks, but I'd prefer to buy some. I shall be needing such a lot."

"All right, I'll fetch you some."

The hotel was small, unpretentious, and it was with a tiny sigh of regret that Clair entered through the narrow entrance and walked up to the reception desk. It would have been so nice for her parents to have stayed with Shane, in that luxurious homestead with all its flowers and its high wide rooms. It was strange, but as yet she herself had never been inside. She would never enter it now. Shane had intended arranging some entertainment for her father and mother, he had said, and Clair had no doubts about the entertainments being on a lavish scale. Well, all that was ended before it had begun. She and Shane were sworn enemies – or so she surmised. But she was in for a surprise – although, at this moment, she did not know it.

"I'm sorry, but we have no accommodation at all. We're booked up for the next three months."

"Booked up?" Clair stared disbelievingly at the dusky woman behind the counter. "But who would be filling the place up like that?"

"We have ten rooms only, and one family alone are to take up four of them – they come in another two weeks and will stay for over a month."

"Is there anywhere else where I might get a room? It's only for sleeping; my parents will stay with us during the daytime and evening."

The woman shook her head.

"Usually there isn't much call for rooms, so no one bothers to let them."

"Oh, dear, whatever shall I do?"

"I'm very sorry, I'm sure," said the woman, and returned to the novel she had been reading.

After having bought Jean's notepaper Clair made her way back to the vehicle. But as she passed along the familiar tree-shaded main street she saw to her dismay the tall figure of Shane coming towards her. Dressed in tight-fitting trews and a red and green checked shirt, he looked exactly what he was, an outdoor man, a man whose life was spent with nature.

She would have escaped if she could, but as this was not possible she put on a mask of cool composure and returned his greeting with a forced smile.

"Shopping?" he queried in the pleasantest of tones.

"No. I've been trying to get my parents fixed up at the hotel."

He frowned.

"The hotel's full up."

"Yes, they told me so."

"I thought it was all arranged that your mother and father were to stay with me?"

"You surely don't want them now?"

He stood looking down at her for a long moment, then shook his head impatiently.

"Why shouldn't I want them?" he asked.

"Well. . . ." Clair licked her dry lips. "After our quarrel. I mean, you wouldn't feel very happy at putting up my parents, would you? – not after our quarrel."

"That's the second time you've mentioned a quarrel. I wasn't aware we'd had one."

"Of course we quarrelled!"

"You chose to argue with me, but that's not a quarrel. And, my little one, I must warn you here and now that I'll not put up with that behaviour when we're married. Your husband's will shall be obeyed."

She looked up into his stern grey eyes, her own violet ones misty from the tears which lay behind them. She was depressed, wanted nothing more than to go to him, and have him put his strong, protecting arms around her. It would be heaven!

"I think you're teasing me," she accused. "And I must say I don't understand why you're not displaying anger – or something," she ended vaguely.

"Would a show of anger have profited me anything?" he queried, a touch of amused sarcasm in his voice.

"No, I expect not." She had wanted to be calm and as composed as he, but already she was uneasy, feeling inadequate beside his air of nobility.

"Shall we have tea again?" he suggested.

"That would be nice."

"There isn't any need for this awkwardness," he assured her. "We're still friends, and don't you ever forget it!" The last few words were emphasised, and in them there lay a threat. Without thinking Clair said what was in her thoughts.

"You'd make an abominable husband! You'd be so bossy and overbearing it wouldn't be possible to live with you."

"No?" in some amusement as they began to walk on, making for the café. "Well, my little one, let me warn you that I'll not look kindly upon desertion. I'd bring you home, and when I did I'd tan your backside until you begged for mercy – and then I'd give you a bit more for being a coward."

Swift colour fused Clair's cheeks. She wished she could find some acid retort, something that would burn into him, but as she could not find anything she remained silent.

"I only want a drink of tea," she was saying five minutes later when Shane asked her if she would like some cakes as well as the tea. "I'm not hungry."

"You've upset your nervous system." He gave the order and continued, "No more worrying over your parents. They'll come to me as arranged."

"You're very kind."

"I'm not. I'm brutal and demanding. You had proof of that at the barbecue."

"Please," she implored, colouring again, "don't ever remind me of that!"

"You want to shrink right into yourself just because you responded to my lovemaking. Foolish child! You ought to be thanking your lucky stars that I didn't go any further— No," he said shortly, holding up his hand in a gesture of admonishment, "don't you dare tell me I couldn't have gone further or I might find an opportunity of showing you that you're wrong. You were in the mood for love, my sweet, and looking back now I realise I would have gained more by taking you completely. You'd have been so scared you'd have married me within a couple of days!"

"Oh, I wouldn't!"

"Let's get on to a less personal subject," he advised gently. "You're such a baby, and are so easily disconcerted. I've said I'm a brute and it's true. When are your parents coming?" he then asked keeping to his word and changing the subject.

She told him the date, and the time of the plane's arrival. He nodded and promised to meet them.

"I want to go too," she began.

"Of course you do. I shall call for you at nine

o'clock on the morning of their arrival. Don't keep me waiting or we won't be there on time."

"I'll be ready," she promised, and then, after a small hesitation, "Is Jean's friend staying with you as well?"

"Jean asked me to have the girl, so I'm doing so. It'll save you all a good deal of trouble."

"Yes, and especially as Sharon's wedding is so soon. She's having to have time off to see to her clothes and to do things at her new home."

"Jean's selling out to me, as you know. I'm sorry she's leaving; she could have made a good thing out of Ngumi Farm."

"But aren't you pleased that you're going to get it, after wanting it all this time?"

"I'm pleased at acquiring it, but I didn't want to acquire it from a grand person like Jean. Mr Lumley, yes, undoubtedly I'd have been pleased. He was a nuisance to have for a neighbour; for one thing his cattle were always in my maize and his poultry scratching up the vegetable garden which was, at that time, the pride and joy of one of my most trusted men. When he threatened to leave me I naturally went over to Ngumi and played hell with its owner."

"It was because you were sworn enemies that he refused to sell out to you. You should have tried to apply a little more patience and tact."

"No, I should not. I'm glad he refused to sell out to me." Picking up his teacup, he took a long drink.

"Glad? But why?"

"I should never have met the girl who's going to become my wife."

"Oh . . . I see."

"You see that you're going to be my wife?"

"No – you know very well what I meant!"

"Are you going to be sensible and marry me?"

"You have my answer. It stays."

"And you have my assurance that we shall be married – and that stays."

Clair shrugged her shoulders.

"It's time I was going," she said. "It's my turn to make the evening meal."

He glanced at her hands and frowned.

"I should have sent you a boy to do the chores. It's not too late now," he added, and promised to send over Joseph, who was used to being inside the house rather than outside. Clair protested, saying they could not take one of his helpers when they were perfectly capable of doing the work themselves; she was answered without delay, and in that imperious tone she had heard him use on several previous occasions. "You'll have him all the same. I don't want my bride to come to the altar with hands that are disfigured by hard work!"

She gave a deep sigh, opened her mouth to remind him that she had no intention of marrying him, but closed it again. He'd never be convinced until she left Ngumi with her parents, bound for England and her home.

He called for her as promised and they drove in

quiet companionship for several miles, traversing what was for Clair entirely new terrain, although it was often similar in aspect to the bushveld around Ngumi Farm. But this was sometimes more like a wilderness, its silence and its loneliness, the sort of dreary solemness that pervaded the valley where flowed the tributary river now that the rains had come ... all combined to make one wonder how man had come to live here in the first place.

The desert aspect went and a more green vista took its place. It was a brilliantly clear morning and when the sun shone on a green cultivated field it seemed far brighter than when it shone on the parched land. The valley was now well wooded, the lower slopes of the hills clothed with herbage, and so everything was softened, made noble by the mingling of the diverse features.

"We'd better discuss arrangements," said Shane at length. "I take it you're having your parents at Ngumi all day, and they'll come over to Linyanga each night?"

"Yes. I was intending to ask what time you went to bed, so we could make sure they're in in time."

"They'll have a key."

"That's very good of you, Shane."

"I do have some redeeming qualities, then?"

"You have many redeeming qualities," she told him seriously.

"Thank you, Clair."

"Now you're being sarcastic!"

"A little."

"I hope you won't be sarcastic with my parents."

"I most certainly won't! On the contrary, I shall obviously be on my very best behaviour with the people who are shortly to become my in-laws."

"You won't be convinced that I'm determined to remain a spinster all my life."

"When is this glamorous young thing expected to arrive?"

She started, shaken by the abrupt change of subject.

"Tomorrow, but she's coming in a car, which she brought over on a ship."

"A lady of means, it would seem?"

"She's been living in Spain with a rich aunt. The aunt died and left her a fortune."

"Lucky girl. And so she's indulging in a little travel?"

"That's right. She found out that Jean was here and naturally chose to visit her."

"So we're to have three new faces around? Yes, we must arrange a round of activities and entertainments. I myself shall give a party, at which we shall dance – and probably announce our engagement—"

"Shane, please be sensible!"

"I forgot, you don't want an engagement. You want a rushed affair, so that I can't change my mind. But you'll have to be prepared for some gossip, sweet. There always is the first wagging tongue that sets it all off."

"Sets what off?" inquired Clair innocently, and Shane burst out laughing before he answered her.

"The suggestion that it was a 'had to get married' affair. People will stare at you, expecting little junior to appear before his time. However, if that's really what you want, my love, then that's what you shall have." He paused, sent her an amused glance and then continued to tell her about the entertainments. There would be at least two Club dances while her parents were here, and perhaps a yacht race. There were polo matches if they cared to attend and there was tennis at the Club. "It's more than likely that some of the others will put on barbecues and other events, so your parents should have a most enjoyable time."

"I'm ever so grateful to you, Shane. You've made everything so easy for me."

"It's a pleasure, Clair." He was serious now, and he slowed down to a stop. "I love you, Clair, and it's natural that I should want to make your path smooth. I'm expecting to become your husband, no matter what you say to the contrary." He turned, and she did not move her face, even though she had plenty of time to do so. His lips were cool, and gentle, his breath clean and fresh, his touch was like a heady wine in its effect upon her. It would be so easy to say yes, she would marry him. She rather thought that, eventually, she would say yes.

This admission was made so simply that its impact on her was scarcely noticeable. She loved him; she knew for sure that he would never let her down, either before or after marriage. So what was the sense in turning him down? She was a fool even to think of it. But she would not say yes just yet. She wanted to be free when her parents came. At the dance. . . . Yes, she thought, excitement taking full possession of her, she would agree to Shane's making the announcement at the dance.

The plane came in, swooping down like a gigantic bird. Soon the reunion was over, the introduction had been made and, after the odd glances which passed between Clair's parents following their examination of the handsome man standing beside their daughter, they were all in the big, comfortable car and making for the little homestead which Clair had described and which she always mentioned in her letters.

"We're dying to see it, love!" exclaimed Mrs Duncan affectionately. "You and the others seem to have made a little paradise out of it."

"Oh, no!" protested Clair. "I can see I've misled you. It isn't anything much at all. It's just that we've worked hard on it and so, to us, it's very attractive in comparison to what it was when we came."

"And Mr Neville's your nearest neighbour, you said?"

"So you wrote home about me?" teased Shane and, over his shoulder, "Shane's the name. We don't bother with surnames any more."

"Shane. Well, I don't recall that Clair ever referred to you as anything other than Mr Neville."

"She wouldn't," was Shane's rather dry rejoinder.

"Oh . . . is there something subtle in that?" Mrs Duncan wanted to know.

"You and Father will be staying at Shane's house," interposed Clair, determined to change the subject. "I did tell you in my last letter."

"Yes, you did. It's most obliging of you, Shane, to put yourself out for us. We're exceedingly grateful to you."

"Don't mention it," returned Shane. And under his breath he said, so that only Clair could hear, "I have an ulterior motive, but as yet they're in ignorance of it. Do you think they'll welcome me as a son-in-law?"

"You didn't have an ulterior motive when you first made the suggestion that they could stay with you."

"Changing the subject all the time— Sorry, Mr and Mrs Duncan. We had no right to whisper." But he did whisper, just to say, "You're wrong. I did have an ulterior motive. You see, I made up my mind to marry you a long time ago, that was why I was so anxious about your deciding to give that bounder up altogether."

She understood it all, had done ever since she had learned that he wanted to marry her. Well, he would soon know that he had won. She would have told him quite soon, but as she saw that he was perfectly cheerful, and brimming with confidence, she did not consider it necessary to provide him with the information yet.

"This is a lovely country," commented Mr Duncan, twisting his head around and eyeing the land-scape appreciatively. "No wonder you girls wrote so glowingly about it."

"Sometimes the scenery's not so attractive as this," warned Shane. "The bushveld can be very monotonous, especially in the dry season."

"Yes, I've heard about that. You have no summer and winter, just a wet season and a dry one."

"That's correct," was Shane's reply. He chatted on, but sometimes he would be silent, affording Clair and her parents an opportunity to talk among themselves. Clair was happy, and it showed in her eyes and her smile. She had noted those initial glances from her parents, anxious glances, but not so anxious as they would have been had she not told them of her decision not to return to Keith. They had known nothing of his plea, and this was as well, since Mrs Duncan would have been even more anxious about her daughter, troubled lest she make the mistake of marrying Keith, despite what he had done to her.

Ngumi was reached at last; Shane left immediately he had unloaded the luggage from the boot of his car.

"I'll let you have a key in the morning," he promised Mr Duncan. "I'm afraid it's been mislaid, but my houseboy will have found it by now. I shall be up when you come tonight – in fact, as I rarely go to bed before midnight I expect I shall be up most nights. However, don't think you have to be in any particular time. I'm letting you have the key so that you'll be free to come and go as you like. Goodbye, Clair. I shall probably see you some time tomorrow."

"What a perfectly charming young man he is!" exclaimed Mrs Duncan when they were mounting the steps to the verandah. "You girls are very lucky having such an exceptional neighbour." She was in the living-room now, and glancing around appreciatively. "My, but this is cosy! Stephen dear, how would you like a little place of this kind? You did say you'd consider a little farm one day. Do you suppose we could rent one like this?"

Glances passed between Jean and Clair. Jean's mouth went tight. She passed the matter by, adopting a charming manner towards Clair's parents. She had always been popular with them and they had given her affection, remembering that she was an orphan.

After the couple had washed and changed tea was served on the stoep. Mr and Mrs Duncan were delighted at the idea of eating outside, in the fresh air.

"I could live here," Mr Duncan was declaring the following morning at breakfast. "It's so warm and balmy, even at this time of the morning, and in November!"

Both he and his wife had enthused over and over again about the bedroom they had been given at Watsonia Lodge. It overlooked the main gardens, with their fountains and statues, and beyond, the wooded little river valley and away past this the low line of rugged kopjes.

"We might have booked in at the best hotel in South Africa," was Mr Duncan's comment. "Shane must be a very wealthy man."

At a quarter past three in the afternoon the third guest arrived. Christal. . . . How well her name suited her, thought Clair. She fairly scintillated, with her shining hair of palest gold, her lovely colouring and perfection of features. Her brows were dark and curved, her eyes a vivid blue framed by long curling lashes. The wide mouth was rosy, the chin pointed, the neck long and arched.

"Crikey!" whispered Sharon when Jean had taken Christal into her own bedroom for a wash and change. "She's like something out of a film!"

"Flawless," returned Clair. But now she was not seeing the girl reclining gracefully in one of Shane's chairs. She was seeing her looking rather uncomfortable, because Shane would not be showing any interest in her. But Clair was in for a shock. Shane appeared to be more than a little attracted to the girl and when, at the barbecue arranged by a young couple who farmed close to Bill and Sandy, he deserted Clair for Christal, Clair's whole evening was spoiled. Jean, noticing what was happening, seemed to be secretly enjoying some kind of satisfaction.

"Are you all right, dear?" Mrs Duncan was a little disappointed that Shane was not taking much notice of her daughter. She had watched him with Clair on several occasions and had seen sufficient to invest her with an optimism that Clair might just win the godlike creature for a husband. But what chance had Clair against that lovely girl he was with at the moment? "You seem to be a little – sad?"

"I'm not sad, darling!" It was an effort to appear bright and gay, but Clair was determined not to give her mother any room for anxiety. She had suffered more than enough of that a few months ago. "I'm thoroughly enjoying myself!"

Sandy came up and was introduced.

"Have you seen Jean?" he wanted to know. "I've searched everywhere for her."

"She was over by that fire – where they're cooking the pancakes, or flapjacks or whatever you call them." Mr Duncan pointed and Sandy went off. Clair saw him again, with Jean, and they were strolling hand in hand!

Christal was with Shane, but when he went off somewhere she came over to Clair and her parents.

"Isn't this cute? Eating out and meeting so many new people." Her voice was silky; it seemed an alien part of such perfection. "Of course, I've been to barbecues before, but in England. Invariably you all have to rush into the house at some hour of the evening, escaping from the rain."

"We've had barbecues and it hasn't rained," put in Mrs Duncan. "It all depends on how lucky you are."

"It's precarious, though. Here, one can be sure of the weather."

"We have the most violent thunderstorms," Clair

informed her. "If one came now you'd be soaked before you even reached the homestead."

"Homestead. Isn't that an attractive word? Shane's homestead's absolutely lovely – but I suppose, Clair, that you've seen it many times?"

"Only from the outside."

"Is that all? Oh, well, I must ask Shane to have you in for a drink one evening."

"*She* must ask him!" spluttered Mrs Duncan when the girl had gone, hurrying away to Shane as soon as he reappeared. "Who does she think she is!"

"Shane's guest, Mother, just as you are."

"I'd never take it upon myself to say he must invite someone in for drinks!"

Altogether the barbecue was not a success as far as Clair and her parents were concerned. Try as she would to deceive them, Clair had obviously not succeeded, because she overheard her mother say,

"Our little girl's unhappy, but I don't know why – not yet. Do you think she's fallen in love with Shane?"

"No, I shouldn't go worrying yourself about anything like that, love. Clair's only just getting over that other affair, so it's highly unlikely she's in love again."

"I thought at first that Shane liked our girl enormously. But since this Christal came he's only had eyes for her."

Clair drifted away, desiring to be alone. She felt so unhappy she could have wept. If only Christal had not come. . . .

"But Shane has asked me to marry him, so he must be in love with me—" Clair was no longer convinced, and the more she dwelt on the whole situation the more a certain picture emerged – the picture of a broken engagement. Yes, had she said yes to Shane when first he proposed, she would have now been engaged to him.

"And when Christal arrived he would have transferred his affections, and I would have been jilted – not at the altar, it's true, but jilted."

She set her teeth together, in order to stop their chattering, for she was very cold, cold in every limb and muscle. Even her heart was cold. But she had had a narrow escape; always she must remember that and be thankful. It was a miracle that she had held out against his persuasions. He himself must be thanking her for refusing him.

He came to her at last, smiling urbanely and asking, with a sort of cool politeness, if she were enjoying herself.

"Of course! It's marvellous!"

He looked at her keenly, with his dark grey eyes. There was a strangeness about him, as if he were making a tremendous effort to remain where he was. Did he want to kiss her? Clair's heart thudded with expectation. All was dark in that little shrubbery over there. . . . If he *did* want to kiss her—

"Shane darling! There you are! I wondered where you'd disappeared to! I'm awfully tired. Please take me home." She tucked an arm in his and he turned to look down into her lovely face. A smile appeared on his and he nodded his head accommodatingly.

"I'll take you home," he said, and with an abrupt inclination of his head for Clair, he walked away, his companion trotting to keep pace with him.

"Take me home," whispered Clair, the burning tears gathering at the backs of her eyes. "*Home.*"

Already the girl was calling Watsonia Lodge "home". Already she and Shane were intimate enough for her to call him darling, and to tuck her hand possessively into his. It would not be long before *their* engagement was announced . . . perhaps it would be at the party which Shane was giving, in three weeks' time.

Wandering further away from everyone, Clair at last gave way to tears, weeping as if her heart would break. It seemed impossible that she had suffered like this twice. This was like a nightmare from which she must awake. Shane *had* been sincere— Yes, but that was before he had met Christal. Had he not implied that the glamorous girl would be his choice, as it had been with his father? Christal was lovely as well as glamorous. Her figure was perfect. Yes, they would get together permanently; Clair was fully convinced of it.

And they would in all probability announce their engagement in the near future.

CHAPTER NINE

THE Club dance was the next function after the barbecue, and Clair was intending to wear a lovely white
dress that her mother had bought for her and
brought out, along with several other presents. It was
of thick satin-like material, high at the throat and
draped from there downwards rather in the style of
the classical robe of ancient Greece.

"You look adorable in it!" exclaimed her mother.
Clair smiled, but she was recalling that once Shane
had used the word "adorable" when flattering her
smile.

There was no doubt about Clair's looking lovely in
the gown. It would be the most outstanding one at
the dance, Sharon declared, and even Jean remarked
upon it. Jean and Clair were still a little cool with one
another. On Clair's part it was retaliation because
Jean was often not nice to her at all. But ever since
that evening when she had seen Jean hand in hand
with Sandy there had been a slight softening of
Jean's attitude towards Clair. Clair could not say
whether this was due to the fact of Shane's having
shifted his attention to Christal, or whether it was because of some understanding which had grown up
between Jean and Sandy. It certainly seemed significant that Sandy had been looking for her, and that,
later, he and Jean had been strolling hand in hand.

But Jean had remained uncommunicative and Sharon had decided that there was nothing of any importance between the two.

"Bill would have mentioned it if there had been," she said.

"Perhaps Bill doesn't know."

"Could be, I suppose."

"It would be rather nice if Jean found a husband." Sharon had looked hard at her.

"You've been glad for me, love, and now you're willing to be glad for Jean – in spite of the way she's been treating you. What about yourself, Clair?"

Clair had reddened, and looked down at her hands.

"There isn't anybody for me here, Sharon."

"Shane ... I could have sworn, once, that he cared for you. Jean thought so as well—" Suddenly Sharon had broken off, a slow whistle cutting into her words. "So that's why she insisted on Christal going to Shane's house to sleep! Jean was jealous of Shane's interest in you!"

Because she could not be deceitful about this, Clair nodded in agreement and said,

"Didn't you guess, Sharon?"

"No, I didn't – although I now see that I should have done so. But how dastardly! How unutterably mean!"

Clair passed her tongue over her dry lips.

"Shane and Christal would have got together in any case. They're alike – what I mean is, they've both got poise, nobility. They're both perfect physically.

It was inevitable that they'd get together."

"I wish she hadn't come here!"

"You'd have liked Shane and me to – to . . .?" Clair broke down then, and the next moment she was weeping in her cousin's arms. Soothingly Sharon murmured,

"Don't, love. You wrench my heart when you cry like that. You did it after Keith, and I went home and cried myself; it was agony."

"I'm sorry." Accepting the handkerchief being offered to her, Clair dried her eyes, and her cheeks, then dabbed at the front of her cousin's blouse. "I'm all right now, Sharon. Thank you for bearing with me."

The Club grounds were bright with lights, and alive with people coming, parking their cars, then moving towards the clubhouse itself. All the ladies were in evening dress, the men in dinner jackets. Waiters in white coats conducted the guests to their tables.

"I wonder if we shall sit with Shane?" Mrs Duncan wished for nothing more than that her daughter, attired in that lovely dress, should sit where Shane could see her – all the time. And she was not to be disappointed. All her satisfaction shone on her homely features when she found herself being conducted to a rather large table at which were already seated five people – James and Elsie Fowler, Shane and Christal, and a young man whom Clair had met several times at the functions she had attended. His name was Martin Brookes and he rose, as did Shane and James, as Clair and her parents came up to the table.

Had Shane arranged this? wondered Clair. If so, was it out of politeness to her parents . . . or was it the desire to have Clair herself at his table? Whatever the reason, the arrangement seemed not to please the glittering girl already sitting there. She scarcely smiled at the newcomers; when her eyes met Clair's she stared arrogantly at her, stared coldly and as if at a total stranger. Clair felt uncomfortable, but she had her parents with her and she felt safe and warm.

Shane was looking at her dress, as he had looked at it when she entered. She did not know it, but his eyes had lighted on her figure long before she reached the table. He had allowed a little exclamation to escape him, an exclamation which Christal had heard, and her eyes had followed the direction of his. Her mouth had tightened, but when Shane remarked,

"What a delightful dress!" she had produced the most devastating smile and replied,

"Indeed it is! It stands out among the rest."

But when she saw how this pleased the man sitting opposite to her she lowered her eyes, for there was a distinctly ugly light in them.

Between courses the guests danced. Shane chose to get up with Clair first, a circumstance that delighted her mother but brought a scowl to the face of Christal. Martin invited her to dance and she accepted, but all the while her eyes followed the figures of Clair and her partner.

"Where did you buy this dress?" Shane, holding

Clair close, allowed a little space to come between them, so that he could look down at the dress.

"It's a present from my parents. Mother chose it. She's quite good at choosing clothes for me, which is unusual, because women want to choose for themselves." She was rambling on, saying anything that came into her head. Shane smiled faintly and said,

"Would you mind very much if I flattered you?"

"I don't understand you," she quivered. "How can I mind if you flatter me?"

"You're so quick to adopt the defensive."

"I promise I won't."

"Then let me say, Clair, that I've never seen anything quite so lovely as the vision of a girl in white, entering the restaurant and walking, with the grace of a princess, towards the table where I was sitting."

"Oh. . . ." She looked up at him, her lovely mouth moving tremulously. Shane caught his breath, and he also caught her to him, possessively. "That was the nicest thing I've ever had said to me, Shane."

"Did it make you happy, child?" He seemed concerned, she thought, and wondered why.

"Very happy." And that was the truth. Everything was all right. Shane still loved her – he must love her to say a thing like that. "I must thank my mother again for choosing this dress for me."

"You must wear it at my party."

"If you want me to, I will."

"I do want you to." Imperious the tone all at once. Clair thrilled to the mastery contained within it. "If you should come in any other I should immediately take you back to Ngumi, take off the offensive garment, and replace it with this."

Clair laughed shakily.

"I believe you would, too!" Her heart was singing. For it was plain that he wanted her to wear this dress for one reason only: so that she would look her very best when their engagement was announced. Yes, he meant to have an engagement, even though he had jokingly agreed to a hurried marriage. But as he had said, the engagement would not be a long one. Clair did not care if it lasted only a week! To be with Shane, to lie in his arms and sleep. . . .

"You're quite right, my little one," Shane was saying in that same masterful way, "I would!"

"I shan't give you that trouble. I promise."

"Trouble?" His brows lifted and amusement lit his eyes. "It would be a pleasure, my love!"

Her cheeks coloured. Shane touched her chin and she resisted.

"You're blushing."

"I might be."

"Let me look!" Her face was forced up, but it was not Shane's eyes into which she looked. It was Christal's . . . and they were dark with venom. Clair shuddered and looked away. Shane, unaware of those vicious eyes to one side of him, did no more than tilt his partner's face up again. "Yes, you are blushing – and not for the first time tonight." He bent his head and lightly brushed her lips with his. Clair trembled as he drew away, and her lips trembled too. She started to smile up at him, caught those eyes again, eyes full of hatred, and she shivered so violently that Shane drew her close to his heart and asked in tender accents if she were cold.

"No, I'm not."

"You shivered."

"I don't know what it was," she lied.

"Let's go back to the table and eat."

The next time he danced it was with Elsie Fowler, and then with Clair's mother, who protested that she could not dance but was taken on the floor anyway. Christal was the last to be invited to dance and she rose with a faintly haughty sweep, taking up her dress in one hand and gliding from her place at the table, her dark and glinting eyes seeking Clair's face as she did so.

But on her return she was smiling, and so was Shane. Clair glanced at him; he caught her eyes and held them for a brief moment before transferring his attention to James Fowler, who was talking about the yacht race to his wife and Martin.

After dinner there was dancing proper, in the main ballroom, and again it was Clair whom Shane chose to dance with first.

"Are your parents enjoying their stay?" he began conversationally when Clair remained silent, just following his steps, and content to be in his arms.

"Enormously. They're bemoaning the fact that their holiday is more than half over already."

"Time passes quickly," he mused. "Are you taking them to Pretoria?"

She shook her head.

"Mother's content to stay around here. I think she'd like to live here if Father could get a little farm. He's always wanted one, but whether he'd give up his work or not I couldn't say. He's often talked of doing so, but you know how it is – security's the most important thing."

"It is, indeed."

"Perhaps, when he's retired, he might consider a farm."

Shane merely nodded his head and for the next few minutes they danced in silence, Clair feeling as if she were treading on air and wondering how she could be so foolish as to have thought that Shane could so easily transfer his affections from one girl to another.

Before the evening was over they took a stroll in the grounds; Shane steered her towards a little shrubbery and she was reminded of the night when he had kissed her so passionately, using – in his own words – a callous method of finding out whether or not she loved him. This time his kisses were gentle, but still passionate, his body demanding, but in a tender, intimate way. Clair smiled at him in the moonlight, her lips parted, inviting even yet another kiss.

"You're so lovely, Clair. I shall never tire of taking my fill of your sweetness." His tender caress on her cheeks sent thrills right through her body, his lips on hers were ecstasy. This was love, in all its tenderness and desire, its demand and its fulfilment.

She thought: I've never loved before. What was

between Keith and me was a shallow, insubstantial thing which would have died quickly, leaving nothing, not even a memory.

The night was warm and balmy, the African sky clear and velvety dark; the stars too were clear, diamonds and more diamonds stretching down to the very horizon itself. She remarked on this startling clarity, expressing astonishment at the length of her vision.

"Sometimes it is like this," he told her, his cheek touching hers. "So clear that you feel you could pick out every single star." His head turned; his lips found hers in a long and tender kiss. "You haven't said you'll marry me, little one, but I take it that your surrender is complete?"

She hesitated; she knew not why, since all she wanted to do was please him. Yet before her vision rose the picture of him with Christal – especially the picture of them together when she had called him darling and requested that she be taken "home".

As yet Shane had offered no explanation for that little scene which, to Clair's way of thinking, should never have taken place between a man and a girl other than the one to whom he had so recently made a proposal of marriage. She was guarded, but not by her own desire. Warnings sounded in her brain, but she would rather have not heard them. They told her of the possibility which was still present – the possibility of Shane's being so attracted to the glamorous Christal that his emotions would carry him – as they had carried Keith – to a point where he could not help himself.

And if this should happen then he would naturally have to follow where his heart and his desire led him . . . towards Christal.

If only she weren't staying at his home. The very thought of the girl's being taken home by Shane in his car — as for instance tonight when the dance was over — was like a weapon pressing into Clair's heart and mind. The darkness of the bushveld through which they had to drive, the moon and the stars above, the sweetly-perfumed breeze drifting into the car through a half-open window . . . all these combined to create a most romantic atmosphere, and who could blame Shane if he stopped the car along the lonely road, stopped to kiss the beautiful creature at his side.

Shane was speaking now, murmuring to her, asking her to say she would marry him. Something snapped within her and she twisted away.

"I can't give you my answer tonight!" she cried. "Wait a little while."

Astounded, he made no move to take her in his arms again; he merely stood towering above her trembling figure, his mouth suddenly tight, his eyes hard as steel.

"I believed," he said icily at last, "that we had it all settled. It would appear that I've been taking too much for granted."

She thought of her decision to let him announce their engagement at the dance he was giving; she felt sure she would keep to that decision. Yet she could not tell him so, not just now. Imploringly she looked up at him, into a face remote and cold as a statue.

"Please try to understand, Shane—"

"Do you understand yourself?" he broke in harshly.

She shook her head despairingly. Only a moment ago she had been in heaven; now she was in the very depths of misery. And it was all her own fault.

"No, Shane," she whispered, "I don't understand myself."

"Isn't it time you made some sort of effort in that direction? How do you expect me to understand you if you don't understand yourself?"

"It's the past experience. . . ." She had not meant to say that; it was out before she knew it. Shane drew an angry breath and for a moment she thought he would shake her. But his hands dropped again to his sides and he made to walk away.

"If you continue to class me with that cad, then I feel we have no more to say to one another."

"Shane – oh, no, I—"

"Let me take you back to the ballroom," he cut in, his voice like a whiplash. "I have no intention of indulging in profitless arguments."

"Shane, please listen! I didn't mean—"

"Give me your hand! It's rough underfoot."

She obeyed, scarcely able to stem the tears that were trying to force their way through from the backs of her eyes. Was this the end? If so, she alone had brought it on.

"If you would listen?" she began desperately. "I might be able to explain."

No response; Shane was taking strides twice the length of hers and she began to skip in order to keep up with him. They took little time to reach the clubhouse where, with a stiff little bow, he said good night, and left her.

Jean at least was satisfied by the news that Clair was definitely intending to go home to England.

"I had a feeling you and Shane might get together," said Jean, and her voice was more amicable than it had been for the past week or so. "I know you were intending to return to England with your parents, but later I felt sure you would change your mind." She paused, examining Clair's pale face. "Whatever it was has fallen through, apparently?"

"Yes, it has."

"He asked you to marry him – you said so."

"I also said I'd refused."

"Since then? Have you not had a change of mind?"

"I did, yes, Jean," answered Clair wearily. Her mind told her to say something cutting to Jean, to tell her to mind her own business and cut out this questioning. But she was too unhappy, too steeped in sheer misery to have any wish for trouble with the girl who, until recently, had been such a dear and true friend to her. Jealousy had caused all this, had destroyed the friendship, and it was jealousy that had put Clair where she was now, since it was her own jealousy of Christal that had taken Shane from her.

"But you've had another change of mind, more recently?"

Clair stirred restlessly.

"Look, Jean, please don't make things worse for me. Shane loved me and asked me to marry him. I was afraid of being jilted a second time. It was foolish; as Sharon said, it was a million to one chance. But as I've said, I was afraid. Shane persisted; he continually teased me about my refusal to marry him, but at the same time acting as if we *would* marry, and quite soon. His method worked and I came round to the point where I wanted to marry him—" She stopped, and unconsciously put a hand to her heart. "I love him, Jean, and I still want to marry him. But it was Christal who came between us. Her manner with him, the way she linked her arm into his. She – she called him darling and asked him to take her home. . . ." Clair's voice trailed away as she made pause to think. Jean, standing there with an impassioned expression on her face, seemed fascinated by the hand which was held to Clair's left breast. "On the night of the Club dance we went out into the grounds, and it was then that the parting took place. Previously I had decided to let him announce our engagement on the evening of the dance he's giving for my parents. . . ."

Again she stopped, her bright, tear-filled eyes having taken in the spasm of pain that had twisted Jean's features when Clair had mentioned the announcing of their engagement. It was plain that Jean would have suffered the pangs of sheer misery had she been there and heard an announcement like that. Clair's heart went out to her, for even in her own unhappiness she could find compassion in her heart for Jean. "As I was saying," she continued, because Jean was waiting to hear the rest, "I'd come to the point where I would welcome an engagement, but somehow I couldn't tell him so. It was because of my fear that he would fall for Christal, that it was possible for him to do so because she was going to his home every night to sleep. On the night of the Club dance I made the fatal mistake of mentioning that past experience. He flared with anger—" Clair spread her hands and added in a voice choked with unshed tears, "That was the end. Shane saw me back to the ballroom, then left me. I haven't seen him since."

A small silence followed.

"It's only five days since the dance. It isn't long; you can't be sure he won't come round."

Clair looked at her.

"He won't come round, Jean. I know he won't."

"And so you've definitely made up your mind to go home?"

"Definitely. I couldn't stay here and see him married to Christal."

"*Married to Christal!*"

"He's sure to fall for her now, isn't he?" Clair wanted to add that both she and Jean had lost Shane so perhaps Jean would now be her friend again, but she hesitated and the moment was lost.

"I'd sooner see him married to you than to her!" Jean's eyes were blazing; Clair had never seen her in such a mood. "He could never marry a girl as artificial as Christal! She's not his type – how can she be if you are?"

Clair frowned at her, a deep puzzlement taking possession of her. There was something most peculiar about Jean at this moment.

"Shane once told me he liked glamorous girls. His father married one, and was in love with her all his life. That's what makes me believe he'll eventually marry Christal."

"No! Oh, God—" Jean put her face in her hands, shaking her head all the while. "I didn't mean it like that! This isn't what I planned. Christal! The sly and unpredictable little bitch!"

Clair, who had been standing in the middle of the room, took a horrified step backwards, away from Jean, and gasped,

"You asked Christal to flirt with Shane, so that he'd transfer his affections from me...?" It was Clair who was shaking her head now, shaking it vigorously, as if she would remove some horror from her mind. "I knew why you'd let her stay with Shane, that you *hoped* she would oust me in his affections, but I never believed you could actually *engineer* it. You asked Christal to flirt with Shane," Clair repeated, but this time it was a statement, not a question. "Jean, how could you do such a thing to me?"

"I don't know, Clair. I was crazed with jealousy!" Dropping her hands, Jean looked at her through dull and lifeless eyes. "I couldn't bear to see you married to Shane, to live here and see you all the time. I imagined children, eventually coming running over to Ngumi, children that looked like you and Shane. Clair, can you even begin to understand the depths of my feelings?"

Clair stood there, shaking her head. Words came to her lips but were never spoken — angry, accusing words which would not have helped at all.

"I can understand," she said stiffly at last. "You seem to have forgotten that Keith threw me over for another girl."

"What have I done to you?" cried Jean in anguish. "And it's all rebounded on me — or it will have done if Christal marries Shane."

"Neither you nor I will be here to see them together."

"But it wasn't what I wanted to happen! I had no idea that Shane would be attracted to anyone as glamorous as Christal; I believed I was safe in asking her to do her act with him. All I intended was for him to have a light flirtation with her—"

"Just until I'd accepted that I myself had no chance with him?"

"Yes, I own to it. But to think he might marry her—!" Jean broke off and Clair heard her teeth grit together. "What a sly one she is! Do you honestly believe she has a chance of becoming his wife?"

"I do." But Clair would say no more. "It's time we dropped all this, Jean. What's done is done. Neither you nor I were meant for Shane, so the best

thing we can do is accept that and try to forget him."
She paused, looking at Jean curiously before venturing to ask about Sandy.

"I saw you and him walking hand in hand," she went on, "and I thought there might be something in it."

Jean shook her head.

"If it was left to him there would be. As for me – I shall never marry now."

"You won't be in love with Shane all your life, Jean. Time will dim his memory." Clair bit her underlip so hard that it bled. Time would never dim Shane's memory for her. She would love him for ever.

"I expect you're right, Clair, but for all that I don't think I shall ever marry. Certainly I could never marry Sandy."

"He's nice. I wish you could fall in love with him." Deep sincerity rang in Clair's voice and Jean's face twisted.

"You could wish me happiness, after what I've done to you?"

"I understand your jealousy. Yes, of course I could wish you happiness, and I do."

"Sandy knows I don't love him."

"But he loves you?"

"Yes. He suggested moving to England and buying a farm there. I'd been talking about my grandfather's farm and he became enthusiastic. He'd like to set up on his own now that Bill's getting married. Sandy didn't propose to me, but his plans included me; I could tell."

"If he did ask you to marry him—?"

"I couldn't!"

"Later, Jean, you might come to care for him."

Jean was silent, and as Sharon came in a moment later nothing more was said.

"What a lot of work a wedding makes!" Sharon dropped her parcels on a chair and flopped down in another. "However, as I've now spent up entirely, I shan't be able to go to town again! And I'm relieved, I can tell you!"

"What have you bought this time?" Clair wanted to know.

"All sorts of things! Nighties and underwear; two blouses and. . . ." She stopped, looking from Clair to Jean. "What's wrong? You two haven't been quarrelling, I hope?"

Both shook their heads.

"Can I ask you not to tell Sharon what I did?" Jean's voice was low, imploring.

"I shall never mention it to anyone."

Sharon said,

"I see. Something between you two only. Well, to get back to this shopping. The only thing I didn't enjoy buying was a broom and a parcel of dusters which Bill asked me to get for him."

"For you, you mean," said Clair, and she actually managed a laugh. "I expect you'll find pleasure in using them, though. From what I've seen of the furniture over there it needs a good deal of polishing."

"It does! But what can you expect when two men live together? Nothing gets done properly."

Clair looked affectionately at her cousin. She was so happy, so in love. For her everything had run with total smoothness, and Clair was glad for her. She and Sharon had always been the best of friends, and they would continue to be. Sharon had asked Clair to come over for a visit one day in the future and at that time all was well between Clair and Shane. But Clair had kept this to herself, merely saying she would most certainly visit Sharon and Bill in their home. Well, a visit might be possible one day – but Clair felt instinctively that once she had left Africa with her parents she would never return.

CHAPTER TEN

THE little church was packed. Clair, dressed in a long medieval-style gown, looked as lovely as the bride, but the one who stole the show was Christal, her expensive suit, her hat from Paris and her shoes from Italy bringing audible gasps from all the women present – all except Clair and Jean. Jean had been asked to be a bridesmaid but had refused, so Sharon had only one. Sandy was best man, and it was plain that he would have liked Jean to have been a bridesmaid.

For Clair the ceremony was beautiful. She had feared at first that the atmosphere of church and guests, of the organ and the flowers, of the lovely white wedding gown worn by Sharon, would bring back memories so distasteful that she would not be able to enjoy what was going on. But she was pleasantly surprised, since Keith's face never once arose before her, nor his best man coming down the aisle with the note.

The reception was held at the Club, which was less than two minutes' drive from the church.

"Didn't she look lovely?" Clair's mother made this comment, watching her daughter closely as she spoke. "You felt nothing, love?"

Clair smiled reassuringly.

"Nothing, Mother."

"That's marvellous. It really is all over, then?"

"It might never have happened," Clair assured her.

"One day you'll find someone else."

No answer from Clair. She was sitting some way from Shane, but she glanced down the table, for he was very strongly in her thoughts just now. Christal was opposite to him and the two appeared to be talking privately, as they both leant across the table. Would their wedding be next? No use dwelling on the possibility, but this was easier decided than carried out. Soon, though, Clair would be going home, leaving Africa behind, and Shane. . . .

"I mustn't cry," she told herself sternly. "How awful it would be if a tear rolled down my cheek now! Mother would swear it was for Keith; she'd think I'd told her a lie."

At last it was all over and Sharon was back at Ngumi, with Clair helping her out of her wedding dress.

"How very sad that it won't ever be used again." Sharon was fingering one lovely soft fold of lace. "I think I'd like to lend it out, and make the wish that the brides who wore it felt as happy as I!"

"What a beautiful idea. I hope someone will borrow it from you, Sharon."

"You—" began Sharon. "You're not happy, Clair."

"I shall be soon, when I take up my life again back home."

"I wish. . . ." Sharon stopped. She was standing in a long underslip, her eyes on Clair as she carefully laid the white dress across the bed. "I know I oughtn't to bring this up, but, that day when you and Jean had been talking and you promised not to tell anyone what it had all been about, I felt that you and she had been discussing Shane."

"We had." Clair turned to take the underslip which her cousin was discarding.

"You're both in love with him."

"Yes."

"Jean never had a chance; she knew that."

"It doesn't make the pain any less."

"She ought not to have allowed herself to fall for him." Sharon's voice held the merest hint of disgust.

"It isn't always as simple as that, Sharon. You can't help yourself. Perhaps you would understand a little better if I asked you to imagine that Bill hadn't returned your love."

Sharon nodded her head.

"I know what you mean. However, I'd never have been as catty as Jean. She deliberately let Christal stay with Shane. There was room here, and as you said at the time, Shane was willing to lend us a bed."

"Well, it's all in the past now, Sharon." Clair folded the underslip and, going over to the wardrobe, brought out a smart suit of dark blue linen. "It's your wedding day, so you shouldn't be troubling your head about Jean and me."

"I'm so happy that I want everyone around me to be happy, that's all." Stepping into the skirt, Sharon pulled it up and fastened the zip.

"We'll be happy one day."

"I know you will."

Clair watched as the short, perfectly-cut coat was put on.

"You look very smart," she said, handing her a handkerchief. "Do you want the perfume spray?"

"Of course. I'm of the opinion that this particular perfume did a lot for me in the beginning. Bill admits that it goes to his head." She was laughing with her eyes. Clair smiled, recalling how shy Bill had been at first.

"Have a lovely time," Clair was saying a quarter of an hour later when the couple were in the car, ready to drive away. Tin cans of every description and size had been tied to the back of the car, and across the back window the inevitable, "Just married". A huge L-plate had been fixed to the back bumper and all over the car was confetti, sticking because of the oil that had been smeared on the entire body.

Among those who were seeing the couple off were Shane and Christal. The girl never left his side these days, thought Clair, recalling having seen the couple twice in town, and on both occasions Christal had been walking as close as possible to Shane.

"I'd hate a send-off like that," purred Christal. "It's vulgar, in my opinion."

"It's a jolly good send-off," declared Sandy. "If nobody troubles to decorate your car then you're obviously not a very popular person."

"That's one way of looking at it," someone said. "'Bye! Have a good time!"

"Where are they going?" Christal wanted to know.

Her hand was resting on the sleeve of Shane's coat. Clair looked at it – and at the same time Shane looked at her. She blushed, aware that he knew she had been looking at the girl's hand.

"They're touring."

"How dull! I'd have to be going somewhere exciting, like the Bahamas or Miami."

"Bill and Sharon want quietness, and solitude."

Shane glanced at Clair again. She recalled him saying that his ancestors had come to this eastern plateau in order to find solitude and peace.

"You'd think they'd want to go somewhere other than their own country. Why, they can tour around here any time!" Christal's voice grated on Clair's ears and she moved away. Shane's eyes followed her and she hoped he knew why she had moved. How he could stand that voice all the time was beyond Clair's comprehension.

"I've told her what I think about her!" Jean spoke in Clair's ear as the car moved away in a cloud of dust.

"She's under no illusions regarding my opinion of her."

"How did she react?" inquired Clair interestedly.

"She laughed in my face and said it was my own fault, which it was." Jean paused for a moment. "Will you ever forgive me, Clair?"

Clair turned and said impulsively,

"I've forgiven you already, Jean. Think no more about it. I don't think Shane was really for me anyway." This was a lie, but said with the best intentions. Clair considered that Jean had suffered enough. "We'll still be friends?"

"If you want that," returned Jean, and for the first time ever Clair detected a hint of humility in her tone. "I have some news which I think you'll like."

"You have?"

"Sandy's asked me to marry him. So determined, he was, saying he wouldn't take no for an answer. He knows I don't love him yet, but he's willing to take a chance."

"You've agreed to marry him?"

"Yes."

"Oh, but this is great news! I'm very, very happy for you, Jean. And I liked the word 'yet' which you inserted."

"It spells hope. Yes, I believe that eventually I shall learn to love him. We're settling in England, so you and I shall see something of one another."

"You're buying a farm?"

"Yes, in the Cotswolds, we hope."

"When will you be moving to England?" asked Clair.

"Quite soon. Bill's already promised to see about buying Sandy out. Sandy asked him to do so a few days ago – it seems he was more sure of my marrying him than he ought to have been," ended Jean with a grimace.

"Well, it all appears to be working out well." The suave voice came to Clair after she had left Jean and was making her way towards the back stoep. She turned, her face tight and pale.

"What do you mean, Shane?"

"Everybody is happy. I heard about Sandy's proposal being accepted." The voice was dry now, and crisp as ice.

"News travels fast around here," commented Clair.

"Weddings are always occasions for the spreading of gossip."

"So it would seem."

"There's been another little item going around," Shane continued.

"Oh?"

"Another engagement to be announced shortly."

Another engagement. . . . Clair felt as if her body had turned to stone, for every feeling was drained from her. Shane and Christal. . . . It could be no other.

"That – that'll be nice." She could find nothing else to say and she made to walk on.

"Don't you want to know who the happy couple are?"

She looked towards the stoep.

"I know who they are," she quivered, and left him standing there.

Only the party now and then they would be getting ready for the flight to England. Well, there would be a little time left, but that would be taken up in shopping and in a few calls. There would be no time to think; that was the most important fact. The party, Clair had at first decided not to attend, but as her parents were the guests of honour she did not see how she could stay away. In any case, her parents would want to know the reason for her conduct. And so, resigned, but not intending to spend much time on her appearance, Clair put on a dark, brushed nylon dress trimmed with grey lace. It was one her mother had passed over to her years ago, saying she might be able to make a skirt out of it. It looked drab, but what did that matter?

"Darling!" gasped her mother when she appeared in the sitting-room. "You're not going in *that*!"

"What's wrong with it?"

"Everything, you silly child! You can't attend Shane's party looking like a frowsy old rag-bag!" Mrs Duncan was almost in tears, but there was something more than this in her manner. The wearing of the dark dress might have been a major tragedy, from the way she looked at her husband.

He swallowed, and looked awkward. Something strange about him, too, decided Clair. She thought back, to when she had gone up to get herself ready. There had been a sort of inner radiation about her mother then – as if she had won the pools, or had some other good news delivered to her.

"No, Clair love," Mr Duncan was saying, "you can't go in that. Your white dress—"

"That was what I expected her to wear." Mrs Duncan produced a handkerchief and blew her nose. "Shane liked it so much."

That, thought Clair, was the sole reason for her not wearing it. Shane had given her every indication that their engagement would be announced at the party, and he had told her to wear the white dress. Now he was intending to announce his engagement to Christal, so Clair had no desire to wear the white dress.

"I'm all right," she said. "I want to go in this."

Her father tried once again to persuade her into changing, but she was adamant. Her parents looked at one another and shrugged resignedly.

"It's going to spoil it all," wailed Mrs Duncan.

"I agree, but if Clair won't change then she won't."

And so she arrived at the glittering party in the drab brushed nylon dress. Christal was brilliant, like a star that shines out above all the rest. It was as it should be, since she was the chief one at the party – or would be once the engagement was announced, with Shane running second in importance. He stood on the top step of the lovely colonial mansion, receiving his guests. Immaculate in a dinner-jacket and snow white shirt, he looked the acme of noble perfection. Totally masculine, sure of himself, smilingly urbane. But it did seem that his *savoir faire* would desert him when his eyes alighted on Clair. He had already spoken to her parents, as she herself had lagged behind. He turned to greet her with a smile, but then his jaw seemed to drop and the smile was wiped from his face.

"What the devil—!" Just in time he stopped himself and his smile reappeared with miraculous speed as the Club President and his wife came up the steps.

"Elsie, James, good evening."

"Shane – a very good evening to you," returned James heartily. "Looks as if this is going to be one of your very best parties!"

A fleeting glance towards Clair and then,

"I hope so, James. I planned that it should be rather special."

"Given for Mr and Mrs Duncan, I heard?"

"And for their daughter." But this was said through gritted teeth, and spoken after the couple had passed into the house.

"What do you mean by wearing a thing like that?" he demanded of Clair.

"This?" She gripped the front of the dress. "It's all right."

Suddenly he laughed. It made an incongruous sound, but no one inside appeared to notice. Shane grabbed Clair's hand.

"Inside!" he ordered.

"What—?"

"Ladies and gentlemen," said Shane in clear and carrying tones, "I have to apologise to you for a temporary absence I must make. I shall be with you all in about twenty minutes' time—" He looked at Clair, whose face was a mask of bewilderment. "No, give me half an hour. I have an idea I shall need it."

"Shane, what is this?" Mr Duncan's voice rose above the babble that had followed Shane's little speech.

"I'll be back," he promised, and the next moment Clair, having been literally dragged to a side door, was once again swung off her feet and presently dumped into the back of Shane's car. Protests had been ignored; little cries of fear interrupted by such words as, "Shut up!" or "Do you want a box on the ear!"

"Where are we – we g-going?" she faltered, leaning forward to touch Shane's shoulder.

"You have a very bad memory, my little one. I threatened that if you wore anything other than the white dress for my party then I'd take you back to Ngumi and strip you—"

"Strip?" she faltered. "Are you mad?" But her heart was bounding – no, it was dancing, for there could be only one explanation for all this.

"Very sane, my love. And looking forward to the pleasure of undressing you."

"No – oh, Shane, I thought it was Christal you were getting engaged to!"

"I can forgive you for that. In my attempts to make you jealous I probably went too far." He was driving at speed, with no regard at all for the ruts in the road. "But I can't forgive you for wearing a damned dress like this!"

"It was Mother's, and—"

"It looks as if it was your grandmother's!"

"Shane, why have you been so horrid with me lately? It's no wonder I felt you'd changed your mind about wanting to marry me—" Clair stopped, the words jerking back into her throat as she was thrown to one side of the car. "Please be careful!"

"No time. Why was I horrid? Because, after you'd led me on to believe you were going to give me a favourable answer, you turned right around and told me you couldn't marry me! What the devil do you think I'm made of? I decided to finish with you once and for all; that's the reason I was horrid to you, as you term it!"

"I was intending to let you announce our engagement at the party— Oh, Shane, do take care! We'll both be killed!"

"Then why the devil didn't you tell me you were willing to have the engagement announced?"

"Because of Christal. It did seem that you cared for her, so I was afraid that you might jilt me—"

"Rubbish! You've made doubts out of certainties. I once told you to think about those words. The certainty was that I loved you – loved you since the business of the snakebite—"

"All that time!"

"Stop interrupting – and sit back, we're coming to a great hole in the road. Yes, since the snakebite. The doubts were created by you yourself. You couldn't see the certainties because you were too damned busy looking for doubts!" He paused a moment, then went on, "If I don't leather you in about five minutes' time then my name's not Shane Neville!"

But his threat was never carried out. Instead, he took her in his arms immediately they entered the sitting-room and kissed her passionately.

"I don't know which one of us was the greatest fool," he said. "I believe I should have taken you that night, and we'd have been married by now."

She blushed adorably, and changed the subject.

"Did you tell Mother and Father that you were announcing our engagement tonight?"

"I called late this afternoon to tell them. Thought it wouldn't do to spring it on them. I asked them not to mention it to you, though. I wanted to spring it upon you – and you spoiled the whole thing by coming looking like a rag-bag! Little one, you'll have to change your ways. When your husband gives an order it'll have to be obeyed – or else. Off you go and change that dress."

Clair went, thankfully, for she had believed he would carry out his threat and change it for her himself. She hurried, eager to get back to him, glad that Jean had agreed to attend the party after having at first decided to stay away. So she and Shane had the house to themselves for a few precious moments while, between kisses, all the misunderstandings were explained and cast away for all time.

"You look so beautiful," he murmured, taking his fill even yet again of her white-clad figure. "My own, my lovely wife!"

He had her close to his breast and she wanted nothing more. Her lips were offered and he took them, waiting, as he drew away, for that tremulous movement that was always so enchanting.

"I could stay here all night," she sighed. "Shane, beloved, forgive me for being so foolish."

"Forget it, my precious heart. Nothing matters now that you're to be mine." His tender fingers caressed her cheek, following the lovely contours and ending on her mouth. "Like you, dearest, I could stay here all night. But we have guests and we must go."

He kissed her again, took her hand in his, and together they walked out to the car.

 # Harlequin Omnibus

The collected works of Harlequin's world-famous authors brought together in the 3-in-1 Omnibus.

3 Full-length romance novels in each entertainment-packed volume

Three great romances, COMPLETE and UNABRIDGED— by the same author— in one deluxe paperback volume ... almost 600 pages of great reading.

A Great Idea! Harlequin Omnibus. We have chosen some of the works of Harlequin's world-famous authors and reprinted them in the 3-in-1 Omnibus. Almost 600 pages of pure entertainment. A truly "Jumbo" read.

Harlequin Omnibus

**The Harlequin editors have chosen this
superb selection of volumes from the works
of the Superstar authors of Romantic Fiction:**

Complete and mail this coupon today!

And there's still *more* love in

Harlequin Presents...